A Weakness for
Almost Everything

A Weakness for Almost Everything

NOTES ON LIFE, GASTRONOMY, AND TRAVEL

Aldo Buzzi

TRANSLATED FROM THE ITALIAN BY ANN GOLDSTEIN

STEERFORTH ITALIA

AN IMPRINT OF STEERFORTH PRESS · SOUTH ROYALTON, VERMONT

For information about permission to
reproduce selections from this book, write to:
Steerforth Press, P.O. Box 70,
South Royalton, Vermont 05068

Library of Congress Cataloging-in-Publication Data

Buzzi, Aldo.
A weakness for almost everything: notes on life,
gastronomy, and travel / Aldo Buzzi; translated
from the Italian by Ann Goldstein.
p.   cm.
ISBN 1-883642-70-1
1. Gastronomy. 2. Buzzi, Aldo — Journeys. I. Title
TX641 .B893 1999
641'.01'3 — dc21

99-047313

Manufactured in the United States of America

FIRST PRINTING

Contents

INTRODUCTION

A Self-Interview

*M*R. BUZZI, YOU WERE *born in the north of Italy, in Como . . .*

Yes, behind the duomo. My last name, Buzzi, in order to be pronounced correctly by Americans, should be written thus: "Bootsie." My paternal grandparents were the Büzz (Buzzis) of Sondrio, a town even closer to the Alps than Como, and perhaps they were distant relatives of Butz, the dark-brown poodle (*Canis aquaticus*) that accompanied Schopenhauer on his daily walk. Heinzen, Kunzen, Utzen, and Butzen, in the dialect of lower Swabia, are the equivalent of Tom, Dick, and Harry, or as we Italians say, Tizio, Caio, and Sempronio (and Mevio), or, as Dante says, donna Berta and ser Martino.

Before moving to Sondrio the Büzz lived in Rodero, in the Brianza (also in Lombardy), where I can trace them back to Giacomo Antonio de Buzzi, born in 1651.

In a Brianza village stands (or stood) a Trattoria Buzzi, with a handsome inscription over the door. It almost certainly belonged to a relative of mine.

What did my ancestors do in the time of the Crusades? I don't know, and that is the only difference between us common people and the nobility. But certainly they, too, existed, and perhaps allowed others to go, and they stayed home, studying, perhaps.

Do you still have relatives in Sondrio?

Yes, Dora . . . my second cousin. She is a pianist, a piano teacher, she teaches the young Sondrians to play the piano. Her older sister had tiny feet, not like the Chinese women of long ago but still so small that often she couldn't find shoes in her size (this gave her a touch of pride). I think sometimes she must have had to buy children's shoes.

Dora lives alone. She calls me at Christmas with good wishes for the season. Her sister is no longer alive. Nor is her brother, who, after working in a bank for many years, left, bought a farm, and, finally, lived like a farmer (it was his dream) among the animals. Of the great family of the Büzz — seven brothers — almost no one remains.

Sondrio is called Sundri (Soondry) by its inhabitants, who have the good fortune to breathe mountain air on their streets. If, as I'm walking through Sondrio, breathing the good mountain air, I hear coming through a window the sound of a piano, I think that the pianist is probably one of my second cousin Dora's students. I stop, listen, and if I recognize the piece I am even more certain that it is.

This happens . . . once every . . . twenty years . . . or so.

A hunting dog *(Canis sagax)* — belonging to my father, who was a hunter — a female, named Diana, was my first childhood friend. She would have defended me even against a lion.

Diana would sit on the lawn with her front paws spread like a pyramid and her tail wrapped around her body. Her eyes would stare at me intensely, waiting for me to say something in the slobbery language of children and dogs. She understood me and she spoke to me: when she moved her tail, beating it against the ground, she was telling me that Paulìn, my father, was coming.

I would sit on the lawn, too, on a rug surrounded by a wooden fence painted blue, the color for boys. The lawn where we were sitting was on Monte Olimpino, also in Como. The name of the street, like so many other names, has gone right out of my *cabeza*, my poor head. Maybe it's just as well to forget, little by little, what is not essential.

I lived in Como until the age of six. Then I went back to the neighborhood of Como for two years during high school, and this period, which I remember very well, made Como my country, my *patria.*

I went to Como in the morning by tram. Since I didn't have time to go home for lunch, my parents arranged for me to eat at the house of a woman married to an anarchist barber, whose house and shop were very near the school.

The meal was almost always the same: a bowl of meat broth, thin but tasty, with bits of stale bread in it and some grated cheese, and then a small piece of boiled beef and some pickled peppers dribbled with linseed oil, which at that time was the only kind of oil used by the people of Lombardy.

The anarchist was a very gentle, honest man; whenever an important politician came to Como, the police put him in jail for the duration of the visit, and he continued to practice his trade there, shaving prisoners and prison guards. After he was released, he told stories of life in prison, where he was known and treated with respect. His return was celebrated with a modest addition to the menu and a bottle of Bonarda, his favorite wine.

At the end of the meal the barber would thoughtfully drink the last drop of wine, wipe his mouth, rise, give me a pat on the shoulder, say, "Study, study . . ." and go. He'd go down to his shop and, before reopening, take a nap in the chair where he shaved his clients.

My father was a chemist. He went from one industrial plant to another. After a few years we would change city, school, language.

Not outside Italy, but from Lombardy to Tuscany to Piedmont. With a red pencil a Lombard teacher corrected, on papers, completely correct Tuscan expressions. Useless to get upset.

At the end of his wanderings Papa started a laboratory on an old street in the center of Milan. The most precious object in the laboratory was a hank of platinum wire, locked up in a cabinet. I never liked chemistry — perhaps because it was my father's work and sons want to be different — but that hank attracted me hugely, for its value, its mysterious weight, the oddly poor color of the platinum, so different from that of silver.

Do you still have that hank?

It was during the war: of the hank, of the whole laboratory, the whole house nothing remained. So ended my father's career.

Your mother . . .

My mother was German. She had come very young with her family to Prato, in Tuscany, and had studied painting in Florence with a fine teacher. My mother's name was Käthe (Katherine), a name too difficult for her Italian relatives, who called her Ketty. Some small paintings of hers keep me company at home, although it's painful to recall that while she was alive she was not appreciated as she deserved. Who knows where those paintings will be in a few years, I think, if they still exist — in what houses, entrusted to whose hands. Best not to think about it.

One painting shows the window of the room in Via Santo Garovaglio, in Como, where I was born, open onto the looming face of the mountain of Brunate, in shadow, where some black swallows are flying.

She said she didn't know perspective, and she made some mistakes in perspective similar to those that Bonnard, whom she didn't know, had made intentionally. Another picture shows the toy corner of the children's room. There is some toy furniture made by Papa, who had a carpenter's bench in the basement: chest of drawers, sideboard and dining table, chairs, stove with little aluminum pots, bed. This miniature apartment, illuminated from above by the dim light from the window, was inhabited by teddy bears of velvet and sawdust, the work of Käthe.

All the paintings were small, probably so as not to spend too much. Sometimes, if there was a frame smaller than the picture, she cut the picture to make it fit.

The only works she succeeded in selling were some miniatures. She did the first one as a trial: a portrait of Princess Maria Jose of Belgium as a child, painted on a thin slice of elephant tusk. With this she went to an antique dealer who gave her photographs of some customers. She did the miniatures beautifully — a laborious job for her eyes, and certainly the antique dealer paid very little. Still, when she returned home with her reward she was pleased.

The only painter who came (and very rarely) to our house was Costanza, a chemist friend of Paolino, my father, an amateur painter of little merit who, nevertheless, found a way to devote himself to painting and to dress like a painter. Very shy and modest, he talked about painting with Käthe and praised her pictures. He was interested above all in a portrait of his friend Paolino done in the evening while he was reading, with a cigar-end in his mouth, in exact profile, like Piero della Francesca's Duke of Urbino, and illuminated by the reddish light of the lampshade. Was the red too bright? Costanza talked about such problems during dinner, which he appreciated as much as painting. Around eleven he ceremoniously took his leave and did not reappear for several years.

Who are your favorite writers?

All of them, sort of — the good ones. They change with the passage of time.

Do you prefer to live in the city or the country, or by the sea?

I prefer a house in the city, surrounded by a garden that faces on one side the main street and on the other the sea or the country. It's a house that doesn't exist. This house should also look out on a solitary meadow where a donkey, a calf, and a chicken are feeding. Plus a dog, a cat, and a couple of blackbirds.

Would you like to raise animals?

No. I would like to live near many animals. To welcome them, offer them tasty bites, see them live to old age, to a natural death. To see a calf chewing its cud sets my soul at ease. That is, it would set my soul at ease if I could see one. The last calf I saw was at the butcher.

Are you a good cook?

Yes, but now, after so many years, I would like someone to cook for me, by surprise. Not a cook, but one of those blessed women who exist now only in the country, with four petticoats and three aprons. And while she works, while she's making the tagliatelle, I can sit there watching her as if she were a calf chewing her cud, with a glass of port beside me, the bottle, too, a guarantee of the future.

What is your most successful dish?

I find that . . . the apron, as it is worn in the north, is very becoming to women. I can look at it, as at a calf chewing its cud, without getting tired.

What is your favorite dish?

All of them, sort of — the good ones. They change with the passage of time. Once, in the United States, while sitting in the kitchen in front of an electric oven with the light on, and watching, for lack of a calf chewing its cud, some scallops, dusted with bread crumbs and black pepper, cooking on a lightly buttered tray, I said, that is, my host said: "The oven is your television."

It was indeed a show, because the poor mollusks, owing to the extremely high heat, were making little settling movements, as if, at the point of taking on the gastronomically most perfect form, they had regained, for just a moment, life.

"The fact is," I said, "that I have a weakness for scallops."

"The fact," my host responded, "is that you have a weakness for almost everything."

Do you remember the first piece you published? When was it?

It was a marvelous night . . .

A night?

One of those nights that exist perhaps only when we are young. That's not me, obviously. It's Fyodor Mikhailovich . . . the beginning of "White Nights." The first piece I published? Yes, I remember . . . "When the Panther Roars." It came out in *Il Selvaggio*, a literary journal. I included it, with some changes, in my first book, and then, still correcting and cutting, in another book. I've written several books, always writing the same things.

So, according to you, a written work never reaches its definitive form?

A writer (with exceptions, like Carlo Emilio Gadda) continually corrects his works. If Dante had lived twenty years more *The Divine Comedy* would be different.

Is there such a thing as inspiration?

There are the Muses, and without their help it is useless to try to write, nothing good will come out. Comforts, conveniences, even a beautiful view keep the Muses away. When Goethe was writing he deliberately sat in an uncomfortable chair, as he explained to Eckermann. If a writer says to me, "I'm going to Capri to write my novel," I'm dubious; that is, it seems unlikely that that novel (if it's ever written) will be a good novel. I think you can see very easily if a work has been written with the help of the Muses or not.

Are you working now on something new?

I am trying to free myself from the roar of the panther; I wish the calf would come forward to replace the panther.

Do you have regrets?

Of course. For example, not having read many books that I ought to have read. One of the many is *The Man Without Qualities*. Perhaps at the beginning there is something that curbs the desire to go forward. Or one has read something about the author that makes him unsympathetic. Anyway, as I usually do when I break off my reading of a book, I went to the end of the first volume:

> He was surprised by the entrance of the servant, who, with the solemn expression of one who has arisen early, had come to wake him. He took a bath, allowed his body some hurried but vigorous gymnastic exercises, and went to the station.

An echo of this fascinating finale at the station, which invites the reader to take up the book again, appears in a page of Delfini's *Diaries*. But the Italian writer, because of his incurable indecisiveness, has gone even further than Musil:

> I took a shower bath. I washed a handkerchief and a small towel. Then I packed my suitcase with the intention of leaving. At the station, however, *je me suis découragé*. I went and got a shave and then returned home.

Are there other books you regret not having read?

The endless *Ramayana*, the most famous Indian text, which is composed of twenty-four thousand distichs, and is one of the most glorious (it seems) masterpieces of human genius; and — also in India — the *Mahabharata* and the *Rig Veda*; and, moving on to Japan, to China . . . *Je me suis découragé*. Of the famous Arab poet, Amr'ul Quais, I have read only these lines, noted down years ago on a scrap of paper: "Her hand is gentle and her delicate fingers are like the insects that climb on the sands of Zhibi or toothpicks made of ishil wood."

I felt some consolation in reading, in Gide's diary (in his library he had a shelf devoted to books he had not finished reading), of a dialogue between him and Valéry during a meeting at French Radio where they were consultants. Someone mentioned the *Iliad*. Valéry says under his breath to Gide: "Do you know anything more boring than the *Iliad*?" "Yes," Gide replies, "*La Chanson de Roland*."

You asked me who are my favorite writers. It would be easier to tell you who are my least favorite. I am happy to be almost always in agreement with the judgments expressed by Nabokov in *Strong Opinions*, which I've just finished reading. Here is the list, I hope complete, which should help to modify certain classifications:

> Second-rate and ephemeral the works of several puffed-up writers — such as Camus, Lorca, Kazantzakis, etc. . . . *Ulysses* towers over the rest of Joyce's writings, and, in comparison to its noble originality and unique lucidity of thought and style, the unfortunate *Finnegans Wake* is nothing but a formless and dull mass of phony folklore, a cold pudding of a book, a persistent snore in the next room. . . . Brecht, Faulkner, Camus, many others, mean absolutely nothing to me. . . . *Doctor Zhivago* . . . I regard as a sorry thing: clumsy, trivial, and melodramatic. . . . [There are] some others — such as Ilya Ehrenburg, Bertrand Russell, and J.-P. Sartre — with whom I would not consent to participate in any festival or conference whatsoever. . . . Since the days when such formidable mediocrities as Galsworthy, Dreiser, a person called Tagore, another called Maxim Gorky, a third called Romain Rolland used to be accepted as geniuses . . .

Doesn't that seem to you a bit excessive?

No, some of his other opinions I don't share, but these, yes. After giving his opinion of *Finnegans Wake*, Nabokov, who knew the milieu, wrote: "I know I am going to be excommunicated for this pronouncement."

What in your view is the ideal novel?

Today, at my age, it seems to me the ideal model for the novel is the one that Proust wished to write (and did): "A novel full of passion and meditation and landscapes." The illustrious Charles Robert Darwin had a different model in mind. "A novel," he wrote in his autobiography, "is a work of the first rank only when it has some character whom one can love, and if this character is a beautiful woman, so much the better." Above all, he thought a novel should have a happy ending. "There should be a law," he said, "prohibiting them from having unhappy endings." No one excommunicated him.

I know that you were at the Linguists' Club, in London.

Yes, one of the many English schools for foreigners. The place itself was very beautiful: a white neoclassical villa, pleasingly rundown, with a nice garden, in Kensington. (The villa isn't there anymore, it was leveled by bulldozers, which unfortunately work even in London.) I was no longer a boy, but, for that very reason, to sit in a classroom with a professor at the front and fellow students — men and women, many of them young — beside me was a wonderful adventure, which I recommend to everyone, including you.

One must have the time.

One must find the time. I also gave some Italian lessons to English people who were preparing for a trip to Italy, and earned a few pounds which I spent at The Tun of Port, an elegant restaurant a few steps from the Club (it's no longer there, either). The meal ended unfailingly with blue Stilton, oat biscuits, and a glass of port (a wine that many years later became my favorite) served by the young proprietor himself, who was very elegant, always courteous and smiling. He was one of those young Londoners who in the time of Stevenson gathered at the Bohemian Cigar Divan by T. Godall, on Rupert Street, Soho. The proprietor's mother, who must have had a lot of money, had financed that gastronomic venture which was destined to come to a bad end precisely because of the ideal way it was run. As he poured the port into my glass, I saw the immaculate shirtcuff, which, coming out of the sleeve of his Savile Row jacket, displayed an aristocratic gold cufflink. Making the comfort of the neighborhood complete, there was, near the club, and I hope it's still there, a luxurious old public toilet (as to dimensions: a small villa), with the noble sign GENTLEMEN. On foggy nights I would see Sherlock Homes come staggering out the door, under the blue light of a gas lamp, followed by Dr. Watson.

Does one learn English well in those schools?

Not very. To learn it well one has to be the only foreigner in the midst of English people. But what can I say? I spent at the Linguists' Club one of the coldest winters of my life but I have a wonderful memory of it, a great nostalgia.

Is there any other country that you feel a special nostalgia for?

Yes, there is, it's Yugoslavia, where I was for quite a while, for work. It was soon after the war. We often cursed the backwardness, the dirt, the incredible slowness of everything. And yet . . . for the first time I saw Cyrillic characters . . . the icons . . . Russia . . . In Belgrade I usually ate at the Metropole restaurant. Here and there sat some *segnorine*, generally rather pretty girls, in little hats and not at all vulgar, looking for someone to sit at their tables. The waiters brought big tureens of steaming soups, *ciorbe*, a bit too fatty but good. *Bez maste!* without fat! was one of the first expressions to learn. Veal, chicken, pork soups; big oval-bottomed plates with delicious boiled beef swimming in an excellent broth, flavored with horseradish. The customers smoked and drank rakija continually. In one corner a duo (violin and piano) played gypsy music. I still remember a few words from the menu, which was our grammar book: *kùvana govédina sa renom*, boiled beef with horseradish . . .

It's not easy to communicate in those countries.

True, but in the end one succeeds. The maitre d' of the Metropole, who wore a greenish-black Dostoyevskian tailcoat in a dignified manner, knew a few words of French and even fewer of Italian, only enough to communicate, in an approximate fashion, with the Italian customers. When someone picked out on the menu the word "spaghetti" and said "spaghetti," the maitre d' wrote down the order with a flourish and, with a connoisseur's smile, added, "À *la dante*."

One day I went up to Cetinje, once the capital of Montenegro — the country of our Queen Elena (Jela), "raven-haired," as Babel says — at the end of a long road that wound through the wild mountains of the lower Adriatic, where the air smelled of aromatic grasses, rocks, sheep, and goats warmed by the sun.

There was a little Grand Hotel, the former haunt of diplomats from Great Britain, France, Austria-Hungary, and Russia accredited to the court of King Nicholas (or Danilo?) and sent to that isolated post probably as a punishment — as Italians were sent to Sardinia — while in reality it was a prize. The cook, who was very clean, like the cooks in the French restaurants in Petersburg in the time of Gogol, was taking out of the oven a wild-strawberry cake.

Have you ever tried that cake?

He brought it to my table himself: a fine cook, and modest. Today the great chefs have their toques and white uniforms made by famous tailors, their wives circulate in the dining room, dressed similarly . . . I prefer a modest trattoria, maybe with a paper tablecloth, where while eating I can glimpse the cook at work amid the steam of the kitchen, in an ordinary apron, on his head an ordinary toque, which has to serve only the purpose for which it was created: to keep the cook's hair from ending up in the customer's soup, an accident that waiters sometimes react to with amusing remarks. The hair in the soup has had the honor of being cited by Kafka, I don't know if from his own experience. But Kafka was able to describe even things that he hadn't seen, like the Brooklyn Bridge, which he did very well, although he had never been to America.

Are you pleased that your book has been published in America?

Very. It's something that, when I began writing, would have seemed to me impossible. America at that time was a very distant country, unreachable. Luckily it is no longer that way.

How did you eat there?

No problem in New York. If your favorite dish is scrambled eggs, bacon, and beer, as it was for Nabokov, America is the best place.

But I would like to suggest to Americans not to leave anything on their plates when they eat (they all do it, for them it's a sign of good breeding); that is, to take or be served a reasonable portion and to eat it all, even cleaning their plate with a piece of bread, a delicious bite whose existence will otherwise be unknown. It would mean saving mountains of food and garbage every day.

That seems a sensible suggestion.

Yes.

When did you go to America for the first time?

In 1952, on a most beautiful airplane, the *Constellation.* The woman who sat next to me on the plane was an Italian-American doctor. I remember her hair, which was red but tinted yellow to make a pale chestnut color. Her father, she told me, had discovered an excellent green Sicilian olive oil, on Mott Street, in New York. She talked to me about America for a long time. "Lindbergh," she said, "when traveling by plane would go tourist class and put his hat over his face. He lived in Hana, in Hawaii, he washed his own laundry and made his own bed and cooked for himself. For nourishment, during the great flight, a packet of sandwiches was enough for him. After the Vikings and Columbus," she said, "infinite numbers of people have still discovered America."

"It's true," I said.

"Don't join the group. Take my father for an example. He discovered not America but Sicilian olive oil on Mott Street."

So when the airplane, with a light shake, touched down on Vine Land, as the Vikings called it, I knew, in a certain sense, how to behave.

Did you look for that olive oil?

No, because my friend used a very good oil from Provence — golden yellow in color, sold in the most expensive stores, in elegant little bottles hardly bigger than a perfume bottle, and perfect on Boston lettuce: oil, salt, and a few drops of water.

I see that cooking still interests you . . .

Really . . . nothing interests me anymore.

I can't believe that. Listen, a last question. Is there something that you would have liked to do in your life and didn't?

There must be, certainly. That's the final question in almost all interviews. Anyway, to end in a slightly different way, more down-to-earth, as donna Berta and ser Martino would, or Heinzen, Kunzen, Utzen, and Butzen, allow me not to answer the question.

All right. Then we'll end with the olive oil?

Yes.

NOTES ON LIFE

W HAT DO YOU WANT TO EAT?"
"Mineral water."

"Some nice mineral water."

"Cold."

"Cold, of course. Was yesterday's cold enough?"

"Veal cutlet with sage."

"A nice veal cutlet with sage."

"And a chicory salad."

"A nice chicory salad."

"Large."

"A nice large chicory salad. You have chosen well, sir. Oh, what you are looking at is the memorial park . . . from the other war."

"I know. Every plant has a label with the name of someone who died."

"At the beginning, yes, but now the labels aren't there anymore."

"Memory doesn't last forever."

"That's it."

"Avoid ending up on a label."

"That's it."

"Avoid eating salad from the root end."

"That's it."

"And bring me the salad so I can dress it while I'm waiting. Otherwise, if you bring it with the cutlet, the cutlet will get cold while I dress the salad."

"Exactly. Right away, a nice salad."

"And a boiled egg, with the yolk soft, which you were incapable of doing yesterday."

"You'll see, sir, today it will be the way you like: a nice soft-boiled egg, with a nice soft yolk, a nice drop of yolk inside."

"And bring it to me unpeeled. I'll peel it myself. I don't want to see fingerprints on the white. Yecch! The boiled egg is an immaculate food. There's no reason to get it dirty."

"Yes, indeed, sir. I'll bring it with its nice shell intact, on a nice little plate."

"Hurry up, then."

―◦ II ◦―

"Dr. Cesarino Gatto?"

"What?"

"Dr. Gatto?"

"Gatti, you must mean."

"Yes, Gatti. May I speak to him?"

"It won't be easy."

"What?"

"I said it won't be easy to speak to him."

"But is he there or not?"

"It's hard to say with certainty."

"Are you joking?"

"I wouldn't joke about such matters. For many people Dr. Gatti is present."

"Listen, if Dr. Gatti is there please put him on."

"Dr. Gatti was here . . ."

"Was there . . ."

"Yes, he's not here any longer."

"Did he move?"

"He's dead."

This Milan apartment is dark as a tomb. When I move from one room to another I have to turn on the light, when I go out into the street and see the sun I have the sensation of coming out of a tomb. I haven't gotten any mail for I don't know how long; all the mail is for the master of the house, who lives on in the advertisments, magazines, bulletins, and invitations to shows that pile up on the silver tray. No one returns this mail or removes the brass nameplate from the entrance. It's understandable, though. And there are still people who telephone him. This one hasn't finished yet.

"You . . . are a relative?"

"No."

"But for how long would Dr. Gatto have been dead?"

"He *is* dead."

"For how long?"

"For a year."

"My goodness! And no one says anything. We continue to send our publication to the dead, with what advantage to our orphans? You tell me."

"Wait, I see here on the tray, among Dr. Gatti's mail, a pamphlet that may be yours."

"A weekly newsletter."

"I see. Invocations to Saint Anthony of Padua. Saint Anthony, sublime doctor of the Holy Church . . ."

"Pray for us. Yes, that's ours. Don't throw it away, everyone is interested in helping the orphans."

"Saint Anthony, furnace of charity . . ."

"Pray for us. Listen . . ."

"Saint Anthony, rose of patience . . ."

"Pray for us. You still want to joke. Did you see in the envelope the subscription form? Listen, you could take Dr. Gatto's place."

This is too much. I hang up the receiver.

Again the telephone.

"Hello Enrico?"

"Hello . . ."

"It's Iolanda."

This time it's just a mistake. "Iolanda . . ."

"Ah, wrong number, sorry."

What a pity, such a pretty voice. I close up everything: shutters, gas meter, five turns of the key for the front door. The mailbox is full. On the sidewalk, in the sun, that stupid tramp with the overcoat, the umbrella and the bundle, picks his nose with one fat finger, makes a pellet of himself . . . which, in the dark of night, thrown on the parquet of the room, makes the impressive sound of a piece of our own body leaving us forever. Good-bye . . . Iolanda. Enrico must be the usual little shit, one of those self-important types, who establish a family, with children, just to demonstrate that they exist.

⟿ III ⟾

The Great-Grandfather (King Victor Emanuel II), besides dying his hair — which before it turned white had been red, two of the colors of our national flag — was a passionate hunter. One morning, very early, he was climbing a mountain path, followed, a step or two back, by the Great Hunter and, a little farther back, by a group of courtiers elegantly dressed in hunting clothes. Bringing up the rear came servants bearing the necessities for the Royal Snack.

An old peasant was heading down the same path, hauling a heavy basketful of hay on his shoulders. At the approach of all those gentlemen he stopped and withdrew respectfully to one side. The King, too, coming up to the peasant, stopped, and, taking out of his pocket a precious crocodile case, whose clasp was in the form of a massive gold crown, extracted from it a Toscano cigar, one of those made expressly for him by the Royal Tobacco Factory. A member of the Royal Party whispered to the peasant that the red-haired hunter was the King. The Sovereign, benignly, condescended to put the cigar in the pocket of the dear old man, who, although he was hampered by the hay basket and upset by the presence of all those too elegant hunters, found the strength to say thank you with an expression that those who witnessed the scene, although at the moment they smiled like the courtiers of *Rigoletto*, could not forget.

This expression, which by good luck has come down to us, deserves to be reported here.

"Your Majesty," said the old man, "this cigar is the most beautiful day of my life."

⎯ IV ⎯

The bells of St. Paul's Basilica rang without interruption, anything at all was good for distraction — chatter, the radio, the newspaper. When the hairdresser entered for a moment, to get something or simply to be seen, her pink smock, unbuttoned in the back, had the effect of a gust of wind: all the trees tossed, the leaves rustled, dry branches fell to the ground.

A dog came in, hesitating, and looked around. Perhaps he was searching for something or . . . It's not easy to understand what a dog is thinking, perhaps he was simply deafened by the bells. The barber carefully put down his razor, went over to the dog, and, with his arm outstretched, showed him the door. And, as the dog did not obey quickly enough, he gave him a kick. Yelping, numbed, the dog flew out of the shop and everyone smiled with satisfaction.

As soon as the dog was outside, he disappeared among the buses carrying tourists to the basilica — vanished, forgotten. What had driven him to enter the shop, who or what he was looking for, what he would have done if he had found the object of his search, where he was going now, yelping, were questions destined to remain without answers. The tourists, descending from the buses by the hundreds, had probably buried him under the avalanche of their lightheartedness. For them everything is fine: the bells ring joyously, and we are the extras who, gratis, animate the background of the basilica — cutting hair, giving kicks, weeping, gesticulating in the Italian fashion.

It was Saturday, I had to fill out the coupon for the soccer pool.

I go to eat up on the Volpi hill, I'll do the coupon afterward. A dog passes me, walking at a good pace; he knows exactly what he's headed for. In order not to deviate from his precise direction, he just grazes me, and now, suddenly, he stops, one paw raised off the ground as if he were posing for a photograph. What is he thinking? What could have come into his mind to make him stop?

The dog remained on three paws for only a few seconds. His brain had worked — had reflected, pondered, and come to a decision: he made an about-face, quickly retracing his steps and grazing me again, and I could look him in the face, a face not only intelligent, compared to the louts I meet in the bar, but also pleasant.

The *carabiniere* made a sign to me to stop. Inside the little shop was the tailor; he had slid off the chair in a strange way and was being supported under the armpits by a friend. He was staring at me with his eyes wide open. He was looking at me but he did not see me, he was looking *beyond*. "He's in a bad way," they said. "You'll have to take him to the hospital." "But can't you see that he's dead?" I said.

A woman who had come over let out a cry, the *carabiniere* nodded to me to go, immediately . . . to play the soccer pool.

But why not play the pool the other days of the week, in tranquillity, without seeing anyone? The old dog in the trattoria, sitting to my left, looked at me as if he were ready to tell me something. I threw him a piece of bread. He followed the trajectory of the bread with his eyes but did not move. He wasn't hungry; he wanted to speak to me.

The fruit arrived. The dog continued to hang on my words. He wanted to make contact. Ah, if only dogs could speak, or man could bark! The poor old . . . animal had in his life received innumerable kicks, plus beatings, pans attached to his tail, attempts to poison him with meatballs, to burn him alive with gas, as they do in China during the carnival. He, perhaps precisely because of the kicks and all the rest, had a look so penetrating that there was no need to speak. If I made the least nod with my chin he repeated it to show that he did not miss anything I did. Perhaps after all it's a dog's life that gets the best results.

The bill arrived. The money went whistling out of the wallet, leaving in the air a trail of the scent of new money. I had to return to the bar, to do my duty, to play the soccer pool.

The bells of the basilica were ringing loudly.

The barber put down the brush, picked up the razor with three fingers, and began to shave. He had before him the most docile client ever to have come between his hands: stretched out in the easy chair, immobile. Of his face, all covered with soap, only the nose and eyes could be seen. The eyes were closed . . . forever. It was the tailor.

The barber took an old soccer coupon, cleaned the lather off the razor with it, and threw it into the wastebasket.

The row of streetlights, seen in prospect, seems infinite. But if you follow the rule and walk under streetlights without paying attention to them, you reach the end of the row in a flash.

Reaching the end I realize I've simply been daydreaming. I remember now having met an old man so dark and wretched that he seemed to be only his shadow. He was walking in a hurry, on the edge of the sidewalk, stumbling, clutching to his chest a tattered lawyer's briefcase, and waving his right arm in all directions. When he passed close by, without seeing me, I realized that he was speaking out loud, arguing, fighting against a powerful enemy . . . hitting him.

I stopped and followed him with my eyes while he went away as if dragged by the fluttering of his arm, until he disappeared into the darkness.

_ɔ **V** ɔ_

Old Melampus, grown white over the years, sat under the desk. His daughter Diana, completely naked, came in for a moment, as if to see if everything was in order. Immediately after, his grandson Fido entered on four paws.

Fido was the son of Diana; he resembled her in the way that children resemble those who made them: even if they are handsomer than their parents, they are always a kind of caricature of them. Melampus looked at him with irritation; Fido seemed to him a stranger. He felt that our true family is our forebears, not our descendants; just as our true age is not the years that we have lived but those we have left to live.

Of his forebears he had had the good fortune to know, besides his mother, his father, with whom he had happily played many times until one awful day the poor fellow ended up on the highway: he became, so to speak, flatter and flatter, until the asphalt had absorbed him and nothing remained of him but a red mark, fainter every day.

His mother came from distant Germany, from Leichlingen, a little village of tiny houses with their half-timbers in view, with small, many-paned windows and embroidered curtains, majolica stoves and cuckoo clocks. Around the houses were little vegetable and flower gardens and orchards full of fruit trees, encircled by a simple wooden fence with a gate and a mailbox. The dog's bed was near the front door, and painted above the architrave was the year of construction. In the kitchen a fair-haired woman in an apron was preparing bilberries for an omelette, or gnocchi of liver and bread crumbs for dinner. On the windowsill the sparrows pecked fearlessly at crumbs of rye bread. The street that led to the school — where, rod in hand, the master taught — was bordered by cherry trees; when the cherries were ripe the classes went to pick them neatly . . .

I see that my mind has wandered: instead of speaking of Melampus's mother I have been speaking of my own, Käthe. Leichlingen for me was a fairy-tale village, a village that I have

never seen (and I think I've done well in not going to see it), that
I know only from the memories of my mother that were more and
more detailed as the years passed. There remains, on the wall, an
old photograph of the Müller house, with the date over the door,
1791, and a fir tree, because nearby was the forest where the bilberries grew.

A cousin of my mother, Fritz, traveled in Queen Victoria's
India selling German chemical-industry products, and he sent his
cousin photographs and beautiful, chestnut-colored illustrated
postcards showing scenes from everyday Indian life. He lived in a
great chalet encircled by verandas, with twenty servants, each of
whom did, or knew how to do, only one job. Twenty did what
Käthe would always do by herself, for her whole life.

The oldest image of my mother, and also the best, is a photograph taken in Ohligs b/Solingen, in Germany, in the studio of
the photographer Walter Hammesfahr. My mother, who was
around four at the time, is holding a bunch of black grapes in one
hand. She is with her sister Ella, the beauty of the family, and already seems to foresee, with her bright eyes, the life of goodness
and obscure sacrifice to which she was destined.

My mother's best friend was Nera, the daughter of the painter
Simi, her painting master. Until she was ninety (perhaps more)
Nera still had all her teeth, white and healthy. She did not use
toothbrushes or toothpicks or toothpaste, because her teeth were
so close together that food could never get stuck. She lived alone.
In winter she gave painting lessons to young American girls, in a
tower on the Lungarno, in Florence.

One summer we went to visit Nera in Stazzema, a village in
the Apuan Alps, below the marble caves — the marble of
Michelangelo — where she spent the summer painting. In
Stazzema marble is used above all for aging lard.

"Professor Nerina?" they said to us at the hotel. "Not in."

The tables were already set for dinner, way ahead of time. At
every place was a paper envelope with the name of the boarder on
it and a napkin inside. At the center of each table was salt, pepper,

and a little molded-glass boat with toothpicks in it. The shutters were nearly closed, to keep the room in half-light. Out with the flies. We felt like staying there.

We ordered beer. The hotelkeeper sat down at our table. We talked about toothpicks, a subject I know fairly well.

The best toothpicks are made in Japan. They are objects congenial to the Japanese; they seem to have been invented for them. Here at one time they were made by hand by lifers, one by one.

"In thirty years of prison," said the hotelkeeper, "you can make a lot of toothpicks."

The spines of the porcupine were also used as toothpicks, as were goose quills. Trimalcio used a silver toothpick, *pinna argentea*. The wealthy people of St. Louis, Missouri, used golden toothpicks. In Naples it was the custom to go out after lunch with a toothpick stuck between the incisors, to show that there was no lack of meat at the table; that is, chicken. Even an admiral — Admiral Cologno, the writer Carlo Dossi tells us — used to promenade with a toothpick in his mouth. The toothpick was so much a part of his image that when he died he was laid out in the funeral chamber with a toothpick in his mouth.

" . . . in his mouth!" said the hotelkeeper.

After the beer I asked him what the cost of room and board was. It was a reasonable price.

We remained awhile sitting in the chairs, savoring the silence of the deserted dining room. A chicken looked in at the door, and, raising a leg, suddenly turned its head in profile in order to explore the inside. I took a toothpick and examined the point, made not by hand but on a lathe.

"If the grain of the wood is not right," I said, "the point breaks immediately and stays stuck between the teeth. Only the Japanese have the proper wood."

"Shoo," the hotelkeeper said to the chicken.

When we left I was still holding the toothpick in my hand.

In American restaurants toothpicks are not on the table, next to the salt and pepper and the red plastic tomato full of ketchup, but at the cash register. The customer, leaving the tip on the table, staggers to the cash register with the check, pays, says good-bye to the cashier, takes a toothpick from the toothpick dispenser, and goes out of the restaurant, out of the air-conditioning, with the toothpick in his hand. For a moment I thought I was in America. The sun was setting. Under the pines and on the asphalt of the road were strewn many pinecones, but all empty of pine nuts. Getting into the car we heard from afar the bells of Carrara.

Instead of looking out the window I was looking at the toothpick, which I hadn't thrown away. I remembered a meal from many years before, my first meal alone in a restaurant, my uncle's restaurant, my uncle who had not wanted to study, like his six brothers, and had become a hotelkeeper, working his way up from the bottom. For years his main job, which would seem of small importance only to a superficial observer, consisted in circulating tirelessly among the tables of the restaurant in his hotel entertaining the customers with jokes, witty remarks, odd items of news, and, at the same time, helping them as quick as lightning if they needed salt or pepper or a toothpick, or whatever. He supplied them even before they had clearly manifested their desire, leaving them pleasantly surprised. Like everyone who in youth has had a hard life he had many things to teach us children. Once he startled me by saying that according to certain statistics (he liked to give a scientific credibility to what he said) women step on dog excrement and other sidewalk debris more often than men because they do not deign to look at the ground.

That's enough, let the dead rest in peace. This is probably the last time my uncle will peek out here among the living. His face, so cordial toward customers, appears to me blurred by a thick fog. I entered the restaurant. When I was seated before a dish, I did not understand that I was living an exceptional event and ought to be observing attentively in order to remember it clearly now, after so many years. Instead I remember almost nothing, whether it was noon or evening, what I ate, or whether I knew anyone sitting at the nearby tables, among which I saw, with a shadow of annoyance, my uncle performing his usual number.

My uncle treated me to that meal, this I remember. It was encouragement to a young nephew. I thanked him (and I thank him again at this moment), wearily I laid down the napkin on the tablecloth. I took, perhaps to give myself a free-and-easy attitude, a toothpick, and, staggering through the cloud of chatter that rose up from the tables, I reached the door and went out into the square.

⤚ VI ⤙

The Captain's eyes were closed but he wasn't asleep; he was thinking, ruminating, remembering . . . With the toe of his foot he was rocking the rocking chair where he sat, in the shade of the porch of his shabby little villa, in the middle of a neglected garden overrun by weeds. Who would want to laboriously dig up the ground, to cultivate vegetables and flowers? To be bent over for hours pulling out weeds, like his Sicilian neighbor, who had fled here from the Mafia, who made an excellent soup of dried fava beans, and who, as soon as anyone took in hand a hoe or a scythe or a pair of clippers, immediately emerged from behind the boundary hedge to insist that he was doing it wrong and teach him how he ought to hoe, scythe, or prune. For many years the Captain had been in command of the *Verbano*, a steamboat on Lake Maggiore, and now, in retirement, he lived alone, and was almost always sitting on the porch reading the same book or meditating on the events of his life. He concluded these meditations with a few deep "Mah!"s, which, like Big Ben, marked time for his neighbors.

Every so often I went to see him. He told me about the most memorable (to him) events of his life, and often I would listen with interest. Once when I arrived after dinner (he ate very early, as old people generally do, impatient to sit down at the table to enjoy the best moment of their empty days) I saw on the porch table a dish with the remains of some noodle soup. The Captain, who was watching me, shook his head with a grimace of disapproval.

"The days are gone," he said, "when poor Signor Dugnani was around, who knew what eating was about, and invited me to dinner, where a broth was served . . . People today can't even imagine what a good broth is."

I told him that I, too, had known Signor Dugnani and during a certain period had often dined at his house and so I was well acquainted with that broth.

He seemed annoyed by my statement and half-closed his eyes in silence.

Signor Dugnani had got rich at the end of the war manufacturing foil wrappers for chocolates. With the arrival of prosperity he had hired a housekeeper, Signora Olimpia, who was to take care of not only the house but its master — a good man, despite his ability to make money, but rather rough and with a tendency, as I had experienced personally, to ignore at the table those rules of a proper upbringing that constituted the gospel of Signora Olimpia. She patiently tried to teach him to keep his napkin on his lap; to bring the spoon to his mouth and not his mouth to the spoon, not to noisily suck up the famous broth; not to spill pasta sauce on his tie, his shirt, and his jacket; not to stain the tablecloth with wine. All in vain. When, having finished eating, Signor Dugnani expressed his well-being with a belch, Signora Olimpia sent him a glance of reproof that would have made anyone blush. But Signor Dugnani was a difficult pupil. He smiled. If he stained the tablecloth he smiled, satisfied and serene.

Signora Olimpia was from a good family and did not miss any chance to remind you of it, like certain Russian "generalesses" who lived like parasites in the homes of rich landowners. She also oversaw the kitchen, of course, and here she was fantastic. She herself did not cook — her status did not permit it — but when the legendary broth arrived at the table everyone knew that the credit was hers.

"There were little pasta rings in the broth," said the Captain, opening his eyes again. "Little pasta rings. The pasta was brought by a worker from Gragnano, near Naples. The broth was that. That's all. A dish of freshly grated Parmesan was passed around, but no one took any: nothing could be added to that broth. It's strange," he said, after reflecting a moment, "but even when I happened to dine two days in a row at Signor Dugnani's I never saw boiled beef come to the table."

"Perhaps he gave it to his workers," I said. "I remember the color of that broth: a pale orange (saffron, maybe?) with tiny pink reflections (a touch of tomato?), and little specks of fat here and there. It must have been made in the classic way: beef, veal, chicken, and a bouquet garni; surely it simmered for a long time, on a low flame, smiling, as Brillat-Savarin says, a barely noticeable smile, like that of the Mona Lisa."

The Sicilian neighbor, fanatically digging the ground on the other side of the hedge (the Captain once said that he worked like a windshield wiper), straightened up to dry his face, which was dripping with sweat, but instead of going right back to work he stood still, looking at the Captain, as if waiting for something. The Captain was not even aware of him.

"Unfortunately," I went on, "that exquisite broth is now gone forever. Signor Dugnani is dead. Signora Olimpia — who knows where she ended up, keeping house for some other rich bachelor, or perhaps, God forbid, in a retirement home where she will not fail to let the other residents know that she is from a very good family, and that when she was housekeeper for the illustrious Signor Dugnani the dinner guests paid her the warmest compliments for everything that came to the table, especially if it was her famous little rings in broth."

The Captain listened, absorbed. He was no longer sitting in the rocking chair on the falling-down porch, beside the remains of an insipid noodle soup that was brought to him every day from the nearby trattoria Italia, he was sitting at the hospitable table of Signor Dugnani, a very large table in the large dining room. At the head of the table the smiling Signor Dugnani, opposite Signora Olimpia. Out of the kitchen came Bigia, the old family servant, whom the housekeeper had ennobled by reclothing her in a big starched white apron, like the ones you see in Bergman films. Bigia was holding the steaming tureen of little rings in broth at nose height, and as she approached the table she filled her lungs with the perfume of that steam . . .

The Captain wiped his eyes with his red handkerchief, then carefully refolded it and put it back in his pocket. His gaze wandered far away, beyond the roofs, to the sparkling lake in the background, which he had navigated for so many years, in command of his boat. He gazed for a long time. Then he closed his eyes and stopped rocking. I saw a sort of lump of feelings form in his breast, swell, rise into his throat. And out of his mouth came, finally, with a deep sigh, the usual bitter syllable:

"Mah!"

The Sicilian neighbor, beyond the hedge, made a gesture of annoyance and went back to his furious digging.

Another time, after he had been sick, I went to visit him in the evening. He was convalescing, and was again sitting outside on the porch, almost in the dark, in the company of the Sicilian neighbor's cat, who seemed to prefer the Captain's house to his own.

I asked how he was feeling.

"An old man," he answered, "never gets completely well. Young people get sick, but then there is recovery, that marvelous regaining of strength, that hunger . . . because the first medicine the doctor ordered, always, was fasting. Then came castor oil with a cup of coffee, cod-liver oil with the Norwegian fisherman on the label, in a raincoat. You don't remember that . . ."

The cat, with a sudden leap, got up on the Captain's lap, but he threw it back on the ground.

"While everyone was eating, in the kitchen, I stayed alone in my bedroom and listened to the sound of cutlery on plates, a sound that we usually don't even notice. Then I asked everyone what they had eaten, how many dishes, what kind of sauce was on the pasta . . ."

Dinnertime had passed a while ago. The stove of the trattoria was being repaired, and that night the Captain would dine late. Darkness fell rapidly, like a black snow, obliterating the view. Mosquitoes began flying around. We left the porch and went into the kitchen. The Captain turned on the light. He became a yellow man: yellow hair, yellow eyes, yellow whiskers, yellow fingers, yellow cat. It was the effect of the electric light.

I looked at his ears. I remembered something the waiter had said about his father: "Papa is about to go . . . you can see it from his ears . . . they're already half dried up." Even though the waiter's father was still alive, nevertheless, after hearing that sentence, every time I saw an old man I couldn't help noticing his ears. The Captain's were not dry but the lobe was joined to the jaw, which according to some has a particular meaning.

We sat down near the table, covered by an old blue oilcloth. The Captain took a piece of bread from a small metal basket and put it in his mouth. When he was commander of the *Verbano*, which had restaurant service, at midday the boiling-hot smell of the engine room, mixed with the aroma of baked macaroni in tomato sauce from the kitchen, rose from the hold up to the bridge, propelled by the fans. This appetizing aroma he would like to smell again someday, on a boat trip. But he always put it off. At the right moment it seemed to him an undertaking superior to his strength. Once he had got as far as the *imbarcadero* . . .

The rocking chair stopped moving. Alarmed, I looked at the Captain, but luckily the crisis lasted only a moment. "*Imbarcadero*," he said, starting to rock again, "comes from the Spanish *embarcadero*, embark. But the Swiss of Ticino, on the other side of the lake, use a made-up Spanish word: *debarcadero*, which means exactly the opposite. Because for them the important moment of a boat trip is when they get off, when they put their feet on the ground again, while for us Italians it's the embarkation, the adventure."

"And the baked macaroni in tomato sauce," I said. "Did you see the cook from the *Verbano* anymore?"

He shook his head.

"People my age don't go out anymore, you don't meet them in the square, at the bar. They're all at home. It's an order that comes from above."

He pointed to the ceiling with his finger, glancing around as if he had been speaking to different listeners.

"Perhaps," I said, "he, too, is shut up in his den not far from here and at this very moment is having dinner. But if he lives alone, even a good cook loses the desire to cook."

"He was a good cook," said the Captain, "a student of the famous chef Ferrari from the village of Poppino — the birthplace of so many cooks and innkeepers — and the writer Piero Chiara was his assistant as a young man. Another famous cook from those places was Pasqualino Percivalle, who was so fat it took two girls to tie his apron behind him."

The cat, with a leap, landed again on his lap and after circling on itself, pressing its paws on his pants, curled up and closed its eyes. The Captain, forgetting Pasqualino Percivalle, laid his big left hand on the head of the cat, which immediately began to purr.

"He's already asleep," said the Captain, "because he has eaten. A cat does only two things: eating and sleeping. It doesn't get bored; doesn't have evil thoughts, like a dog; it doesn't think, like a horse, or a cow, or a goat. When it stops sleeping it goes off again to look for something to eat. And it doesn't take much. For him this garden is a restaurant."

"Meaning?" I asked.

"Birds."

He said "birds" as if he had said "bread," without any pity for the cat's poor victims, who irritated him because they started singing too early in the morning, waking him at dawn — especially irritating were a couple of blackbirds, who made a nest in his garden, under his nose, moving it every year. No one had managed to discover it, not even the cat. The nest was finally found in winter, when the leaves had fallen, and by then it was abandoned.

On the back of the Captain's left hand, illuminated by the lamp, appeared a tattoo of an anchor, the sky-blue color of veins; probably it was the symbol of a life that in youth longed for adventure. But now the anchor had been dropped definitively in our peaceful harbor, and when occasionally I had tried to learn something about the tattoo, there had been no response.

We heard the gate creak. Then hurried footsteps on the gravel, in the dark. Then someone climbed the noisy wooden porch steps. The waiter from the trattoria came in with dinner, which he placed in silence on the table: three dishes, one after another: soup, main course, and fruit, wrapped in a tablecloth. He laid the table in a hurry, went to the sink to get the dirty dishes from lunch, and with a *"Buon appetito"* in a low voice, barely convinced, headed for the door.

"How's your father?" I asked.

"He's about to go," he said without stopping. He opened the door and went out, closing it behind him quickly, as the Captain requested, to keep out the mosquitoes.

The Captain threw the cat to the floor and sat down at his place. He asked if I wanted a taste. A formality. The sky-blue anchor, having left the cat's head, was now resting on a stale roll. I wished him a good meal while he sprinkled abundant salt and pepper on the insipid noodle soup, I filled up his glass with wine, and went off. In the darkness, as I headed toward the remote light of the trattoria, the Captain's anchor became confused with a tattoo I had seen that morning on the chest of a young man from the village, a young man who was on the dull-witted side. I had met him walking in the woods, shirtless because of the heat.

"What does that red heart mean?" I asked. "A woman? Love?"

"No, adventure."

"And the black ship above the heart?"

"Adventure."

"And those black dots around the ship?"

"Seagulls."

⁓ VII ⁓

The man in the delicatessen on Via Teodosio turned to his distinguished-looking male customers (more or less; even I was among them) with these two words: "Dear friend." "Dear friend," he would say, "you certainly want the best for your table . . ."

One day I said to him that Emmental is written without an "h" and urged him to correct the sign that he had stuck in the cheese, even though the name was stamped correctly on the rind, as I pointed out. I explained to him that in German "Tal" means valley and Emmental (not Emmenthal, with the "h") is the valley of the Emmen torrent, in the north of Switzerland, where this cheese, esteemed and imitated throughout the world, is made. My words did not convince him.

"Dear friend," he said, "let the Swiss write it as they like, but here in Italy this name is always written with the 'h.' All our gastronomes write it that way, and I don't feel like being an exception."

I went to that delicatessen for a very brief period, because that familiar tone right away started to annoy me. Besides, soon afterward the delicatessen closed and of the dear friend I knew no more.

In place of the delicatessen a copy shop opened. I went in to photocopy a letter. The clerk was doing some calculations and did not seem to have time for me. I waited thirty seconds and went out. But in my mind I said: "Dear friend, you can pass your time like the Swiss, that is, as you wish; but, in spite of everything, I think that Emmental should be written without the 'h,' even if our gastronomes and some men of letters put in the 'h.'" I was, as you see, under the influence of the departed dear friend. His anchovies with lemon juice, his *vitello tonnato* dotted with tiny black capers, his Russian salad that was too yellowish red, and even his immaculate white apron — as clean, General Dwight D. Eisenhower would have said, as the teeth of a hunting dog — seem to me now, in memory, infinitely more attractive than photocopying machines. I realized that a natural shop, with very old traditions, had been replaced by an unnatural shop. Another blow to my daily walk.

VIII

How many saints are there? In the Order of Saint Benedict alone there are more than three thousand.

There exist families of saints. Saint Basil of Cesarea, doctor of the Church, is the son of Basil and Emmelia, both saints, and so are his sister Macrina and his brothers Gregory of Nissa and Peter of Sebaste. In the church of Llanpumpsaint, in Wales, a set

of quintuplets are buried one beside the other: Ceitho, Ce-
lymen, Gwyn, Gwyno, and Gwynoro — all saints. Saint Am-
brogio, the patron saint of Milan, and Saint Satiro are brothers
and Saint Marcellina is their sister. The martyred saints Vitale
and Valeria, a Milanese husband and wife, are the parents of the
martyred saints Protaso and Gervaso. Some saints, when they are
alive, give off a very faint aroma, which the faithful call the odor
of paradise, the odor of heaven, the odor of sanctity. "What is this
odor of paradise like?" someone who had smelled it was asked. "I
don't know how to describe it," he answered, "because it doesn't
resemble the scent of any flower or spice on earth." Saint Gaspare Del Bufalo was one of these fragrant saints. In addition, he
walked in the rain without an umbrella and stayed dry. He trans-
mitted this miraculous talent to his secretary, the venerable Giovanni Merlini. We know all about Saint Gaspare because he
lived in a time not very distant from ours: the last century. I know
a relative of his, a pianist who lives in a lovely apartment in
downtown Milan, on the top floor, with a terrace that encircles
the whole place, part of it a flower garden, part for vegetables.
She gave me some arugula plants for my garden in the country.
From the terrace I saw against the sky the travertine statues
crowning the building opposite, and it seemed to me that I was
closer to Saint Gaspare and his secretary. The pianist invited me
to dinner. She brought to the table a marvelous veal shank —
the part from which the butcher usually gets the osso buco —
roasted whole, with a divine sauce.

"A miracle," said a fellow diner after tasting his first mouthful.

He was the director of one of the city's principal museums,
and was used to seeing before his eyes, every blessed day — even,
perhaps, to the point of not seeing them — some of the most famous masterpieces of all time. But that roast, more than a mas-
terpiece, was a true miracle: as when a saint, heedless of a violent
storm, walks from one village to another without an umbrella
and arrives at his destination completely dry. It's clear that from
up there he can also help his distant pianist relative, alone before
a veal shank.

⸺ IX ⸺

Paradise is up there, above the clouds. So said the Russian priest. Then Gagarin, coming out of the little metal sphere of Sputnik (the Traveler), said: "Comrades, during my flight in space I met no one."

There is no single paradise for all of us. Each has his own paradise, which travelers do not enter, and yet cats and dogs, who are not allowed in church, can.

This is my paradise: a road along the sea without traffic, a wide, irregular walkway along the beach, paved with tiles, on which one can walk comfortably even with bare feet. A low wall on the beach side, where one can sit. Small bathing establishments with a few cabins, a few umbrellas, now closed because the sun has set. Small cafés, picture postcards, palm trees not always in good condition, tamarisks. A dog, a cat, a seagull, a lifeguard who is raking the sand. Along the road are low cottages with porches, blinds, nameplates, mailboxes. Through the windows come the sounds and smells of dinner preparations. I see friends of the past go by, dead friends who are no longer dead. Diana, my father's hunting dog, who after so many years recognizes me immediately; and the gray cat I had during the war, who disappeared in the last months (someone surely had taken and eaten her, one of the many unpunished crimes of that merciless time). I go into the house. The table is set, and we sit down, my father, my sister. My mother brings the Klöse to the table, big dumplings that you break into pieces with your fork and that have a sauce of browned butter and milk poured over them. One piece for Diana curled up on my right, one piece for the cat.

My mother's paradise is different. It's in Como. My sister and I are small, our father is young, with a lighthearted smile. At the table Mama's parents are also sitting: Grandfather (Grosspapa), with his carefully trimmed gray beard and a Virginia cigar, bought in Switzerland, sticking out of his jacket pocket, and Grandmother (Grossmama). Here, too, Mama is serving up the Klöse.

Then there are other paradises: my father's, my sister's, grand-father's, grandmother's. And they can all exist at the same time without any trouble. There is also Great-Grandfather Müller's par-adise, in Leichlingen, where Great-Grandmother is serving Klöse to Grandfather, who is a little boy . . . and, finally, the paradise of the horse Cholstomer: a big green field and, in front of him, old Lev Tolstoy, with his straw hat and long white beard, like a mane, who looks the horse in the eye and speaks to him. And one hears the voice of Turgenev: "Listen, Lev Nikolayevich, at one time you must have been a horse."

—◦ **X** ◦—

It was near Christmas, and the street was full of lights lighted even during the day. In a corner of the bar the usual group of customers was listening to the old man's story.

"A lyrebird," said the old man, "was strolling along a street in the city . . ."*

"What street?" interrupted one of the listeners.

"What difference does it make?" said the old man. "If I tell you that, maybe you'll understand better?"

Someone laughed. But meanwhile the unexpected interrup-tion seemed to have made the old man lose the thread of his story.

"What was I talking about?" he said.

"A bird," said his friend Giuseppe.

"Yes," the old man said, picking up the thread, "the lira-bird. A lira-bird was strolling along a street in the city with his son . . ."

"What?" another of the listeners, nicknamed Bis, interrupted him. "A lira-bird was strolling? What are you talking about?"

---

*The lyrebird is so called because the long tail feathers of the male resemble, when spread, a lyre, the instrument of Apollo. The Italian name is *uccello-lira*, and *lira* in Italian is both the musical instrument and the monetary unit, which at one time, when it was worth more, was divided into a hundred *centesimi*, or cents. For the logic of the story, I ask the reader to accept, in addition to the other oddities of this bird's behavior, an Italian-American version of its name: lira-bird.

"If you all keep talking," said the old man, "I can't tell my story."

"Let him speak," said Giuseppe. "Give him a glass of wine, it will loosen his tongue."

The glass was brought, filled to the brim, and given to the old man, who emptied it, wiped his mouth, and began again to tell the story.

"A lira-bird was strolling along a street in the city with his son . . ."

"Where in the city?" came out of the mouth of another listener. (Sometimes the details that seem pointless to the narrator are what interest a listener or a reader. Perhaps they ought to be taken into consideration.) The new interruption roused a general protest. The old man, motionless, gazed at the rim of the empty glass that he held in his hand, waiting for calm to return. It was a while before the silence was reestablished, but finally he was able to take up the story again.

"A lira-bird," he said, "was walking along a street in the city with his son. After he had been walking awhile he stopped in front of a jewelry store."

"And the son?" asked an anxious listener.

"The son? He stopped, too, of course!" the old man said testily. "What do you think he did?" he added, more angrily. But the others urged him to continue.

"The window of the jewelry store," he said, "was ready for Christmas, filled with jewelry and watches. The lira-bird stared closely at the jewelry. The son, too, stared closely at the jewels, like his father. Then the lira-bird moved over to look at the watches. The son, too, moved over to look at the watches. The lira-bird looked at the time shown by a large clock in the center of the window, took out his watch and moved the hands slightly, then started off again on his walk. But the son did not follow him, he seemed nailed to the window with the watches in it.

"'Papa,' he said . . ."

"But what's this?" interrupted Bis again. "Now the birds are talking?"

"At Christmas even the birds can speak," said Giuseppe.

"You're the one who shouldn't talk. Go on," he said to the old man, who continued the story.

"'Papa,' said the lira-bird's son, 'will you buy me a watch?'"

"If my son," said Bis, "asked me to buy him a watch, I'd know how to answer him."

The listeners immediately rose up to silence him:

"Shut up, Bis!"

"We're not interested in your son!"

"Speak when the chickens pee!"

These shouts were enough to make the old man lose the thread of his story again. He went back to looking at the rim of his glass.

"Give him another glass of wine!" said a voice. Again the glass was refilled. The old man remained silent, looking at the full glass. He shook his head.

"What was I talking about?" he said.

"About the lira-bird," said many voices.

The old man seemed reassured. He raised the glass and brought it to his lips.

"Drink!" Bis said to him contemptuously, as if giving an order.

The old man stiffened, then removed the full glass from his lips and put it back on the table. "You've made me lose the desire."

"Damn it!" cried a cardplayer from a nearby table, having angrily thrown a card down on the tablecloth, "did he buy the watch or did he not buy it?"

"No!" cried the old man, just as angry.

"Thank goodness," said Bis. "If we give children everything they ask for . . . What did he say to his son, then?"

The old man stared into Bis's eyes with a gaze that showed a new, unexpected strength. This time, he had not lost the thread, if, indeed, he had ever really lost it before. Having everyone's attention, he took up the story.

"'My son,' said the lira-bird, 'I will not buy you the watch now. I will buy it for you, I promise, when you are grown, when you are a true lira-bird.'

"'But Papa,' said the son, 'am I not a lira-bird?'"

"Precisely," Bis said emphatically. "Isn't he a lira-bird?"

"'No, my son,' said the father." The old man continued to stare into Bis's eyes as he spoke. "'No, my son, no, you are not yet a lira-bird. You must grow . . . still grow. For now,' he said, stopping a moment as singers do to fill their lungs before the final note, 'for now you are only a fifty-cent bird!'"

He burst out in a big laugh of triumph, followed by the others. All except Bis, who remained dumbstruck, like — it used to be said — an ass at the sound of the lyre.

The old man again brought the glass to his lips, emptied it into the "greedy pipes," as the poet says, approved with a grimace of sat-isfaction the quality of the wine, wiped his mouth a second time, and rose, helped by his friend Giuseppe. He said good-bye to his companions, went to the door and out into the street illuminated by a thousand Christmas lights, mingling, with short, dragging steps, like a cross-country skier's, in the crowd that jammed the sidewalk.

Bis followed him, with a baleful eye, to the end. He had diffi-culty believing that he had been taken in by a foolish old man. Yes, foolish. But perhaps, he thought now, perhaps the old man was not foolish, perhaps his own ideas on old age had to be reviewed. Per-haps old men (as Proust, a writer unknown to him, says) are merely adolescents who survive for a sufficient number of years.

⟶ XI ⟵

I threw away my old brown shoes. It's years since I wore them, and they've been resoled twice. It's natural that I feel affection for my old shoes. How well I remember the day I bought them. They were in a window in Lugano, Switzerland, and had a wide toe, the way shoes should be and almost never are. A narrow toe ruins the foot. I went into the shoe store without that sense of unease which I usually feel knowing that the salesperson will make me try on a huge number of shoes and in the end I will not find the right ones. I tried on the shoes, they fitted perfectly. Only one question: to buy one pair or two. With two, I thought, I won't have to think about shoes for the rest of my life. In the end I took only one pair, to leave the future a bit more uncertain. "Would you like a box or a bag?" asked the saleswoman. I asked her how much education she'd had, she spoke so well. Through the shopwindow I could see the square and, beyond, the sparkling lake and some market stalls, and coming out of the store I headed in that direction.

I had to throw my old shoes away. I closed the door of the room and remained alone with my shoes for a while, in silence, as Russians do before going on a journey. In my mind I said a few words of farewell: Dear shoes, thank you for the way you have helped me walk in comfort all these years. I know that in a better world you would be stored in a nice closet, with other retired old friends. Every so often I would come to see you, give you a brushing, and put you on for a few minutes, recalling the days spent together. But one cannot. I have to throw you in the garbage. So the rules of this damned world require. Forgive me.

NOTES ON
GASTRONOMY

—◦ **I** ◦—

*O*NCE, PEOPLE ATE AND drank more (that is, those who
could, ate more, and those who couldn't, ate less). I do not
mean Homeric banquets, or those of Trimalchio, or the tavern
feasts of the four musketeers. General Bisson, Brillat-Savarin tells
us, drank eight bottles of wine at lunch every day. And, as for the
good curate of Bregnier, let's listen again to Brillat-Savarin:

> Although the hour had only just struck noon, I found him
> already at table. The soup and the boiled beef had already
> been cleared away, and those two essential dishes were fol-
> lowed by a leg of mutton *alla reale*, a very good capon, and
> a large salad. . . . Immediately after, a big white cheese was
> served, and in it he opened a ninety-degree-angle breach.

The complete title of Brillat-Savarin's work is *La Physiologie du Goût, ou Méditations de gastronomie trascendante. Ouvrage théorique historique et à l'ordre du jour, dédié aux gastronomes parisiens, par un professeur, membre de plusieurs sociétés savantes.* Marie-Antoine (Antonin) Carême — the most illustrious French chef (his surname means Lent), who was Talleyrand's cook, and later that of the Russian and Austrian emperors and the author of various works, among them the five volumes of *The Art of Cooking in the Nineteenth Century* — passes a severe judgment on Brillat-Savarin (Baudelaire and others also treated him harshly), a judgment that I repeat from Alexander Dumas' *The Great Dictionary of Cooking.* "Neither Cambacérès nor Brillat-Savarin knew anything about eating. Both of them liked robust, vulgar food. They simply filled their stomachs. That's the pure truth. Savarin was a hearty eater. . . . At the end of the meal he was taken up with his digestion. I saw him sleeping." The fact is that Brillat-Savarin — or brilliant Savourain, as Joyce calls him in *Finnegans Wake* — did know how to write.

Carême had started out as a pastry chef, a not unusual beginning for a talented cook. As a very young man, after a long day of work he would stay up at night studying design; occasionally, with the permission of his master, he went to the Cabinet des Estampes, again to study, to seek inspiration for those miraculous culinary inventions (*pièces montées*, the memory of which survives today only in wedding cakes) that would soon make him famous. He said: "The fine arts are five: painting, sculpture, poetry, music, and architecture, whose principal offshoot is pastry."

I believe that Talleyrand was able to invent dishes even without the help of his cook. The *garniture Talleyrand*, a sublime sauce for macaroni — butter, cheese (Gruyère and Parmesan), little cubes of foie gras, and truffles — is a recipe that for its golden simplicity and, at the same time, the princely richness of its ingredients can only have come directly from his brain. In France, truffles are found in Périgord, Talleyrand's real name was Talleyrand-Périgord, and in winter, to protect himself from the cold, he often wore a knit cap of black wool, with two long earflaps that hung down on either side of his face like the ears of a truffle hound.

Besides those who ate less, there were those who ate nothing, like St. Nikolaus von Flüe, who lived in a hermitage for nineteen years without eating. Nicolao della Flüe, as he has been Italianized in the *Canton Ticino*, was a revered Swiss hermit. After abandoning his wife and ten children — who, however, went to assist him when he died — he lived alone in the hermitage of Ranft, not far from the city of Stans, near the Lake of the Four Cantons, the cradle of the Confederation. He couldn't read or write. In the morning he prayed, in the afternoon he visited the priests in the nearby villages. He could be seen walking with a rosary in one hand and a stick in the other. As for meals, he skipped them. In 1841, when civil war was about to break out among the eight cantons that at the time constituted Switzerland, because of the entrance into the confederation of two new cantons, Freiburg and Soletta, the saint succeeded in averting the disaster by sending a conciliatory message to Stans, where the representatives of the cantons had gathered (the Diet of Stans). Relations between a man fasting and a Diet could not but be excellent. Since 1947, Nicolao della Flüe has been the patron saint of catholic Switzerland.

_ᴐ II ᴐ_

The writer who never mentions eating, or appetite, or hunger, or food, or cooks, or meals inspires me with distrust, as if he were lacking something essential. Cervantes, from the very first lines of his novel, lets us know what Don Alonso Quejana, the future Don Quixote, habitually eats on the seven days of the week: at lunch "an *olla* with more beef than mutton, at dinner almost always a meat- or fishloaf, omelette with bacon on Saturday, lentils on Friday, and on Sunday some little pigeons for reinforcement." The *olla* is the principal dish of the midday meal in many regions of Spain: a kind of *bollito misto* — mixed boiled meats — or *pot-au-feu* with chickpeas. *Olla* means "pot." For our

Roman ancestors it was a pottery jar in which the ashes (the memory) of the dead were preserved. The simple everyday *olla* is transformed, on holidays, into *olla podrida* (*potpourri* in French), which literally means "rotten pot" and in the culinary language of Spain means a mixture (perhaps a bit chaotic) of numerous and diverse meats and vegetables: beef; mutton; pig's feet, ears, and tail; partridge; chicken; raw ham; bacon; sausage; and — in addition to the chickpeas — carrots, leeks, onions, cabbage, potatoes, lettuce. It is one of the dishes brought to Sancho Panza's table during his first meal as governor of the island of Barattaria. "That big steaming dish down there," says Sancho, "looks to me just like *olla podrida*, and, owing to the quantity of different things they put in it, I will be able to find at least one to my taste and benefit."

Olla podrida is particularly appropriate for Sancho Panza because it is not haute cuisine but originates, rather, in the obsessions of the starving, who, being unable to satisfy their hunger every day, wish that at least on some occasions they may be able to eat as much as they want of whatever they want.

The first and most extraordinary dish of this kind — one whose preparation recalls, in certain aspects, the casting of Benvenuto Cellini's *Perseus* — was served to the Athenians in 389 B.C. as the festive conclusion of Aristophanes' comedy *The Congresswomen*, and can be defined approximately as a stew of oysters, sliced fish, lamprey, brains, hot sauce, silphium pesto, cheese, honey, leeks, thrushes, pigeons, chicken, mullet, dogfish, hare, pickles . . . One translator has even picked out, among the ingredients of this gigantic *potpourri*, ouzo, the strong Greek anisette.

The name of this ancient *olla podrida*, which I will transcribe into Latin characters to make the reading less of a chore, gives an idea not so much of the tastiness of the dish as of the number of ingredients used for the occasion by the cooks of that popular meal: Lapadotemacho selachogaleokranioleipsaanodrimhypotrimmatosilphioparaomelitokatakechymenochichlepikossy phophattoperisteralektryonopteckephalliokigklopeleolagoiosiraiohaphetraganopterigon.

❧

For cookbooks and books about cooking, perhaps more than for any other kind of book, the saying of Pliny the Younger is valid: "There is no book so bad that it doesn't have something good in it." So many cookbooks have been written by now that it's almost impossible to find a title for each new one. The first cookbook, by the Sicilian Archestratus, had already nearly exhausted the supply, for, as Atheneus tells us, according to Chrysippus it was entitled *Gastronomy*; according to Lynceus and Callimachus, *The Good Table*; according to Clearchus, *The Art of Cooking*; and according to others, *Cookery*.

In periods of decadence the cult of cooking becomes excessive. Pliny complained that a cook cost more than a horse. "Cliton," wrote La Bruyère, "had only two occupations in his life: to lunch in the morning; to dine in the evening." In reaction one reads with pleasure the response given by John Updike to an interviewer who asked him what his most memorable meal had been: "My most memorable meal was lunch with Alfred Knopf, who took me to La Côte Basque when the owner was still Henri Soulé, the famous French chef. I don't remember anything I ate, but . . ."

⟞ III ⟝

When I was small, gold teeth, eyeglasses, and a potbelly seemed to me indications of importance, of beauty. In place of an adult belly, I had a hole, symbolic of the fact that I counted for nothing, had no weight, no authority.

At one, the first bathers began to head for the pensione. The man with the potbelly, gold teeth, and eyeglasses called the attendant over with a nod, and, there in his chair, at the edge of the sea, had a plate of pasta brought to him. A big plate. With tomato sauce. And plenty of cheese.

Perhaps the spaghetti that the attendant served on the beach was not cooked al dente. But what did it matter, with the sort of hunger that comes after swimming? Eyes wide, I followed every forkful that, rolled to perfection, traveled from the plate to the gold teeth; I savored the taste of tomato as if I had it in my mouth . . .

Then came the age of knowledge (of spaghetti al dente), and then the age of crises.

Every so often I am seized with a violent nostalgia for institutional food (school, barracks, office, hospital), a plate of "all wrong" pasta.

I rush to a trattoria somewhere, I sit down, and without even looking at the menu I order spaghetti with meat sauce. I don't ask that it be cooked to order, and this means that it will be overcooked; and I ask for meat sauce — which I usually consider a sauce to avoid — because at that moment it's the sauce I want. I would even like to shout at the waiter: "On a cold plate, please!" but there's no need, the plate will arrive cold.

Once I've devoured the overcooked spaghetti with meat sauce — with pleasure, I have to say — the crisis is over. For quite a long time I will go back to asking for spaghetti cooked to order, al dente, and will protest if it's not.

Something about this story reminds me of the strange case of Dr. Jekyll and Mr. Hyde. If a friend (Dr. Lanyon) came into the trattoria surprising me, greedily eating overcooked spaghetti with meat sauce, the analogy would be even closer.

IV

Over the door of the house where I spend the summer, a modest fresco portrays San Lorenzo holding upright in front of him the instrument of his torture, the grill. Without meaning to, the saint demonstrates the best way to use the grill (in cooking): put the meat on a grill and prop it in front of the fire, not on top of it. In this way, the fat released by the heat doesn't drip on the coals, kindling a smoky flame that gives a bad taste to the food, and one can cook even if the wood flares up, without waiting for the coals to form.

For chicken it is ideal.

Anyone who has tried chicken, or meat in general, cooked this way feels as in olden times the tiger did in India after tasting human flesh: he no longer desires any other.

_⟶ **V** ⟵_

Suetonius is the favorite reading of the chef Allen Lieb, who in 1979 had a moment of great celebrity, thanks to (or through the fault of) the writer John McPhee, a great admirer of his, who published a long profile in the *New Yorker*, keeping secret, as Lieb wished, his real name and the name and location of his restaurant (a secret, however, that could not long resist the hunt unleashed by the press).

Lieb is an interesting cook, not so much because of his professional skill as because of the way he works and the way he speaks about his work: he utterly refuses publicity, he uses his hands more than his implements, loves leftovers, doesn't throw away used matches, never cooks a dish the same way. He says that the most important thing to learn is to go slowly. His conversation, Monselet would say, is nourishing.

At night, after a tiring day, Allen Lieb reads *The Lives of the Twelve Caesars* before going to sleep: emperors greedy for drinking and eating, for sumptuous meals, strange and costly foods, monstrous cruelties. Tiberius, Caligula, Claudius, Nero, Galba, Vitellius, and Domitian all were murdered: strangled or poisoned or their throats cut. Claudius, a glutton for porcini mushrooms, was killed at a banquet by one of his favorite mushrooms cooked with poison. Vitellius, whose voraciousness had surprised the universe — here even the name has a familiar ring in the kitchen — attempted, shortly before he was murdered and thrown into the Tiber, to flee in a litter, "having for companions only his cook and his baker."

Not even "the good Augustus," as Dante calls him, was the model of perfection, as it is generally believed, because that's what we learned in school. Unjustly suspecting the praetor Quintus Gallius of treason, "he ordered his centurions and soldiers to arrest and cruelly torture him, as if he were a slave; and though he did not confess to anything, Augustus himself dug out his eyes, and then had him killed." And: "When Attalus, his chancellor, for fifty scudi showed and revealed to someone a letter of his, he ordered that his legs be broken." And "at a banquet, excited by a burning lust for the wife of an ex-consul who was present with her at the banquet, Augustus rose from the table, led her into the bedroom, and later brought her back to the table, her ears still red and her hair disheveled."

He did not even have the physique of a great man: "short in stature," his teeth "small, few, and decayed." But he could not have been entirely ignorant of cooking, because, "wishing to express a swift and sudden action, he would say, 'Quicker than boiling asparagus.'"

In Rome the name Augustus no longer has anything august about it. It's a name for a counterman: "Hey, Gus, a mocha!"

⚙ VI ⚙

The sculptor Arturo Martini had a poor childhood. He went to school for five years: for two years he was in first grade, for three in second. The son of a cook, he made a true statement about cooking: "Cooking is done by instinct. Someone else may have to taste the soup, I can tell at a glance if it has salt. There is the Artusi" — the famous Italian cookbook — "and then there is also the elusive." That's right. The true cook doesn't taste, he is rather like the pianist who plays without looking at the keyboard.

⚙ VII ⚙

To say the fresher the eggs the better the omelette seems obvious. But Bartolomeo Scappi, the secret cook of Pope Pius V, thought differently: "Take eight two-day-old eggs and beat them, because they are better than fresh ones for making an omelette, since fresh ones make it tough and do not become as pale yellow as the others."

Is it true? It seems an excessive refinement, comparable to another one that Brillat-Savarin mentions: "Have we not in our days seen those who have discovered the particular taste of the leg on which the partridge rests while he is sleeping?"

Or to yet another, among certain super-connoisseurs of wine, who advise anyone who has to bring a bottle up from the cellar to perform the transfer extremely slowly, that is, rest the bottle for a day and a night on every step, in order not to traumatize the contents with a too sudden change in temperature.

⁓ VIII ⁓

The restaurant was entirely of aluminum: walls, ceiling, floor, tables. The plates were aluminum disks. The *carneplastico*, or meat sculpture (in French *viande sculptée*), the most famous dish of futurist cuisine, was the focus of general curiosity. According to the definition (recipe) of its inventor, Fillía, it "consists of a large cylindrical meatball of roast veal, stuffed with eleven different kinds of cooked vegetables. This cylinder, arranged vertically in the center of the plate, is crowned by a layer of honey, and held up at the base by a ring of sausage, which rests" — more or less like certain Roman obelisks — "on three gilded spheres of chicken meat." The *carneplastico* (like so many other dishes that enlivened futurist meals) appeared in the sky of gastronomy like a meteor that shines for a few seconds and immediately disappears, without leaving a trace. Today, rather than a dish of the future we would call it a recipe of Apicius, a fancy of Trimalchio, an antique.

But the futurists had no doubts.

"And of the old cuisine," Fillía was asked, "what will remain standing?"

"Nothing, just some old saucepans."

◦ IX ◦

"Vegetable antipasto: Season bulbs with Apicius' sauce, oil, and wine." That is the beginning of a recipe in the *De re coquinaria* of Apicius, the gastronomic best-seller of antiquity, destined to endure, with infinite revisions, cuts, additions, and repunctuations, much longer than the Roman forum. In it you will find recipes, not easy to interpret, for the most famous dishes of ancient Roman cuisine: baked breast of sow, roast crane in honey sauce, parrot tongues . . . but above all you notice in the recipes the excessively frequent presence of a sauce that the translator calls Apicius' sauce and the author a nasty word, *liquamen*. This sauce is something of a gastronomic mystery: no one has ever been able to explain exactly what it is (some mixture of various ingredients: herbs, spices, vinegar, and fish paste). Apicius does not give us the recipe, too obvious in his day; he teaches us only how to remedy the *liquamen* with laurel and cypress smoke if it starts to smell bad. The best *liquamen*, according to an advertisement that came to light on a wall in Pompeii, was distilled by the firm of Umbricus Agathopus.

"When they are cooked," continues Apicius, who probably dictated his complicated recipes in a very low, hollow voice, characteristic of Romans of all periods, "put in to boil with them suckling pig, chicken livers, chicken legs, and some chopped-up small birds. When that comes to a boil, grind in pepper and lovage. Sprinkle with *liquamen*, wine, and raisin wine to sweeten. When the bulbs have boiled, thicken the sauce with starch."

The desire to eat passes.

After the recipes of Apicius I can understand (just for a moment!) those for whom eating and drinking has no importance. Among them was the writer Lucio Mastronardi.

"Lucio, do you like good food?"

"It doesn't interest me."

"But don't you have a favorite dish?"

"Except for liver, brains, and tripe I eat everything."

"Do you drink wine at meals?"

"No, mineral water."

"Why?"

"Because my wife buys it."

⟋◦ X ◦⟍

I read in Kafka's diaries (August 15, 1913): "Torture in bed in the morning. The only solution to jump out the window." I think of poor Lucio Mastronardi when he went to sit on the edge of the sidewalk, of his life besieged by madness, his double death. He struggled, searching for new ways of writing: if he could no longer write he was finished — nothing else interested him. And yet his inspiration, his talent were not gone. Perhaps, without leaving Vigevano, he had to look at his city from a different point of view. What if he were to start writing a diary?

After his first suicide attempt (November 3, 1974, throwing himself off the balcony outside his living room, on the fifth floor), a lovely daughter was born, and now he'd take her for walks under the porticoes of the piazza; he goes in front, his daughter, whom he calls Maria Bambina, behind.

Throwing himself off the balcony without first looking down, he'd ended up on the trunk of a yellow Fiat parked in front of the house, which had somewhat softened his fall. His shoulder, jaw, and foot injured, he got up by himself, and went to sit on the edge of the sidewalk. It was three o'clock in the morning.

Vigevano, September 6, 1974

Dear Buzzi,

I no longer have the desire to write or anything else. I have been again in the hospital in Voghera; it was a hallucinatory experience. And still I saw little. I'm sending you the outline of the novel: I serve whoever pays me. I began and then the pen fell out of my hand. Enough of writing. There is too much desolation in the world. I would have liked to come and see you but I am still weak.

Yours, Mastronardi

❧ XI ❧

The custom of filling soup bowls to the brim is still observed these days in many modest restaurants, where, however, the food is often anything but contemptible. Broth served this way can be defined as "broth nail-style," an allusion to the waiter's right thumbnail, which is constantly immersed in the broth. (If the bowl were not so full the customer would have the right to protest the stinginess of the portion.) In the same places, at the bar, a glass of wine, red or white, is similarly filled to the top, or, rather, over the top, for the wine rises slightly above the rim without spilling, because of the physical phenomenon of the surface tension of liquids. Skillful as the bartender, the customer brings the glass to his lips with a steady hand, not losing a drop; and usually empties it in a single gulp, winning the right to emit at the end a noisy sigh of liberation.

❧ XII ❧

James Fenimore Cooper, in addition to writing *The Last of the Mohicans* and many other novels that were famous in his time, founded and was the president of the Bread & Cheese Club in New York. The Bread & Cheese Club was also called the Lunch Club, because "bread and cheese" is a synonym for lunch, the light midday meal of Anglo-Saxons (and Greeks and ancient Romans). And in 1500 Gerolamo Cardano wrote: "I always have a lighter meal at lunch than at dinner."

Often his lunch consisted of a white soup of Galen's, that is, chopped boiled leeks, in some of their cooking water, seasoned with oil, vinegar, and salt, and, I would add today, black pepper: a wonderful dish, to which Galen surely attributed curative powers.

I think the soup was called white because only the white part of the leeks was to be used, as all cookbooks advise; even though, faced with the poor leeks, we often haven't the courage to follow that advice thoroughly, and throw a little of the green part into the pot, too; nor is the soup any less tasty for it.

Cardano was the most famous medical man in Europe in the sixteenth century, and, as a mathematician, he showed himself able to illustrate and provide proofs for the solutions of the third-degree equations that, on February 2, 1531, Niccolò Tartaglia had arrived at. In his autobiography, however, Cardano tells of having seen a cock who spoke to him in a human voice, and on the subject of cooking he writes: "The methods for preparing food are fifteen: fire, ashes, soak, water, pot, pan, spit, grill, pestle, blade and back of a knife, grater, parsley, rosemary, and a bay leaf." Lombroso considered him mad.

Springs is a pleasant place near the sea, not far from New York, with large forests where one still meets, as in the time of Cooper, deer, wild rabbits, turtles, squirrels, foxes, and raccoons with black rings around their eyes, who venture out at night to root around in garbage cans.

The last whale to be caught in its waters was caught in 1907: it was fifty-seven feet long and yielded two thousand gallons of oil. The last Indians in the area, the Shinnecock, having by now left the pages of Cooper's novels, show off in summer with native dances. The Mohicans, on the other hand, have disappeared completely from the face of the earth. The last of the Mohicans, as Cooper tells it, was called Uncas (Agile Deer) and died valiantly. Thanks to Cooper we also know the next-to-last of the Mohicans, who was called Chingachgook (Great Serpent), and was Uncas' father. Their ability to orient themselves in the densest forests, and in the dark, was legendary. Indeed, not many years ago in Springs an Indian, Steve Talkhouse, said to a white man who offered him a ride in his car: "No, thanks, I'm in a hurry," meaning that, by way of paths through woods and fields that only the Indians knew, he was sure to arrive at his destination before the man in the car.

No dish from Indian cooking has remained in the local cuisine: a stroke of luck, since the Indians, from a culinary point of view, are undoubtedly the least gifted people in the world. But one local dish is at least curious: graveyard stew, which is usually given to people who are very ill. It's a soup of bread and milk, easy and quick to prepare: toast a slice of good bread, spread it with butter, put it in a soup bowl, add salt and pepper and pour over it a cup of milk that is very hot but not boiling. For one in good health, an excellent soup; for a sick person up to date with local traditions, a decisive experience.

A group of Shinnecock Indians had followed my words in silence. But now one, the old chief Shining Canoe, opened his mouth: "It's not true that nothing is left of our cooking. Succotash is an Indian dish."

In fact, he was not wrong. Succotash is an American Indian dish made of corn and dried beans cooked together, today reduced to a side dish and refined by substituting for the dried beans cut-up green beans (and butter).

"Squaw dish" — egg, bacon, and the usual corn — "is also an Indian dish," another added.

"You're right," I said. "But anyway it's not a big deal."

Shining Canoe coughed and stood up solemnly: "God has given them enough but they want everything. That's how it is with the palefaces."

Having uttered these words — taken, like the following, from *The Last of the Mohicans* — he headed with springy and silent steps toward the forest. "The others followed him one by one in that order so well known as to have merited the name 'Indian file.'"

❧ XIII ❧

Immediately after dinner Kafka went to bed until one o'clock. At one he started writing; at four or five he threw himself back on his bed until it was time to get up to go to the office. He described his ideal way of living and working in a letter to Felice dated January 14 and 15, 1913:

> I have often thought that the best way for me to live would
> be in the innermost part of a very big, locked cellar, with
> everything necessary for writing, and a lamp. Something to

eat would be brought, but the food would always be far away from the place where I was, beyond the outer door of the cellar. The movement of going to get something to eat, in my dressing gown, walking beneath the vaults of the cellar, would be my only walk. Then I would return to my table, I would eat slowly and with concentration, and I would immediately begin writing again.

(Max Brod, in his biography of Kafka, says, "When it came to certain writers, like Hebbel, Grillparzer, Kafka loved their journals more than their works: at least so it seemed to me." It does not seem to me irreverent to think the same of Kafka: that is, that his diaries and letters are his best writings.)

He was a vegetarian and did not pay much attention to eating. He does recall, in his diaries, a New Year's Eve dinner, modest but not lacking refinement, "with salsify and spinach, accompanied by a glass of sherry"; a dinner "of strawberries"; another dinner, in Berlin, with "rice à la Trautmannsdorf" — a sweet, the French *riz à l'impératrice* — "and a peach." Of Milan he recalls an apple pie eaten in "the courtyard of the Mercanti," and beer that "has the smell of beer, the taste of wine."

The name Kafka — again, it's Max Brod speaking — is of Czech origin, and in its correct spelling, Kavka, means, literally, "crow." If it were not such an unattractive bird, I would say that it recalls Kafka's shadowy face. "The flesh of this bird," writes a naturalist of the past century, "is repulsive, but it provides an excellent and very healthy broth."

⟜ XIV ⟞

An utterly unpredictable signboard that points out how far certain fantasies can go appears in the following verses, taken from Baudelaire's "Bouffoneries":

A lively tavern
On the road from Brussels to Uccle

You who are crazy about skeletons
And gruesome emblems
To spice your pleasures
(Even plain omelettes!)

You old Pharaoh, Monselet!
At this unexpected sign
I thought of you: À *la vue*
Du Cimetière, Estaminet!

—◦ **XV** ◦—

Bread is in decline everywhere. One no longer says, "Good as bread"; we will end up saying, like the English: "Good as gold." To try and find out why, I question a baker in the doorway of his shop.

"Maestro, are you officially qualified as a breadmaker? Did you study in a school or did you learn from a master of the art, as the best painters, sculptors, and architects used to?"

"I learned from my father. Today, in the city, you need a diploma."

"People don't complain because the bread isn't as good as it used to be?"

"No, they only want the bread to be white."

"Why is natural yeast, which makes better bread, no longer used?"

"Because with natural yeast the job takes longer: you have to work the dough several times."

"Did you know that the ancient Egyptians kneaded the bread with their feet?"

" . . . ?"

"Also, at one time people used to stamp on the grapes with their feet to make wine. Our forebears used their feet more than we do. As, moreover, monkeys still do."

" . . . ?"

"Is a wood-burning oven better than an electric or gas oven?"

"Of course, because the coals give the bread a special smell and taste."

"Is it true that, as some bakers have told me, wood-burning ovens are forbidden by health regulations?"

The maestro removes from the wall his regular license to operate a wood-burning oven and shows it to me. "No, the end of wood-burning ovens is due to the difficulty of getting the wood. No one goes to the woods anymore to cut it, and anyway it would cost too much."

A fat old man, but fat without seeming prosperous or jolly, had stopped a step or two away from us and seemed to be following our conversation closely.

"See," I said to the baker, "bread is a subject that interests everyone. This man represents the man in the street." He had, to be precise, a knapsack on his back. "If the making of bread interests him it means it's something important. Right?" I said, turning directly to the man with the knapsack.

The man seemed to brighten, and drew from his pocket (a torn pocket) a red card, printed, and politely handed it to me.

> Dear Ladies and Gentlemen. Nature created me a deaf-mute and my only means of existence is the generosity of my fellows. I turn therefore to the kindness of your heart. A thousand thanks.
>
> *Beatus ille homo*
> *qui sedet in sua domo*
> *et sedet post fornacem*
> *et habet bonam pacem!*

‿ XVI ‿

"What did you have for lunch?"
"Pastina in broth . . . little butterflies. And cheese."
"And tonight?"

"Tonight osso buco with frozen peas."

"Fruit?"

"I don't know . . . an apple."

"What kind of apple?"

"Delicious. And a couple of glasses of wine."

"A sweet?"

"No, that's enough. Sunday: profiteroles."

"As an alternative to pastina in broth?"

"Sometimes fettuccine: with butter, or else with tomato sauce. Never meat sauce."

"Why?"

"I don't like it much, nor does my fellow lodger."

"What does your fellow lodger do?"

"He's a chauffeur . . . for an industrialist."

"Do your schedules match?"

"Yes, pretty much."

"What time do you have dinner?"

"Seven-thirty."

"A liqueur at the end?"

"No . . . almost never."

"Is the pepper in a peppermill or already ground?"

"Already ground."

"Can you recall a special meal, out of the ordinary?"

"No."

"Truffles?"

"It's been awhile since I had them: it must be . . . twenty years."

"Where did you last have them?"

"In a trattoria, on a cutlet."

"Do you have a nap after the meal?"

"I don't have time."

"The landlady, does she eat with the two of you?"

"Yes. She brings a tray and serves. If something is left it's eaten the next day: sautéed rice, meatballs . . ."

"Fish?"

"Very seldom. Once she made a fry of shrimp and squid."

"When was that?"

"I don't remember."

"Coffee?"

"Not always. When one likes."

"Toothpicks?"

"I don't use them."

"Are the chairs cushioned?"

"Yes."

"Comfortable?"

"Enough."

"The wallpaper, what's it like?"

"Flowered, in faded colors."

"Are there pictures on the walls?"

"Yes, a scene of Milan: Launderers' Lane. And two paintings of flowers."

"Oils?"

"Yes. At least . . ."

"The pastina in broth is always butterflies?"

"Butterflies . . . yes . . . that is, also little rings, little stars . . ."

Recipe for the boarding-house pastina in broth:

Bring the broth (watery and also greasy) to a boil in an aluminum pot that's not perfectly clean. Throw in the pastina. Call a friend on the telephone and stay on the telephone twice as long as necessary for the normal cooking of the pastina. Turn off the gas, and when the soup is almost cold bring it to the table and serve it in cold soup bowls, saying "Bon appétit!"

"Same to you."

～ XVII ～

Some advice on how to dress a green salad, which is often heard with indifference and seldom followed. And yet it's good advice: oil, salt, and *a little water*. The water doesn't dilute the taste of the oil, in fact it brings it out. After washing the salad don't take all the water out of it by centrifuging it in a wire basket or in a towel; that bit of water remaining constitutes, with the oil and salt, the perfect seasoning (also for fennel, celery).

When this theory was put forward in an aristocratic club on Jermyn Street, in London, "whispered cries" (if by this expression one gets the idea) rose from the mouths (those that were empty at that moment) of the diners: "Unbelievable! That's odd! Ominous! By Jove! Preposterous!"

But, when with some difficulty extra-virgin olive oil was found and things had gone from theory to practice, other "whispered cries" captured the general appreciation: "Terrific! Fantastic! Fabulous! My goodness!"

Fun at the dinner table is indispensable to good digestion. The court jester sat at the king's table for just this reason. A wise institution, and the inverse of today's working lunch, an obviously unwise institution, unless we consider jesters our fellow diners.

⌐ XVIII ⌐

What is the best way to write a recipe?

To this question a definitive response has not up until now been given.

Should we use the confidential imperative "Put on the stove…," or the generic imperative "Let us put on the stove . . . ," or the still more generic "We put on the stove . . . ," or the present indicative "I put on the stove . . . ," or the exhortative future that Gadda uses in his famous recipe for *risotto alla milanese:* "You will put on the stove . . ."?

And as for amounts and times: mathematical precision, "twenty grams," "a half liter," "seven minutes"; or housewifely approximation: "a pat of butter," "enough," "a glass of wine," "a pinch of salt"? "And with whose fingertips?" said the Italian writer Prezzolini. Nutmeg, for example, should be used in very tiny amounts: a dash is too much — a shadow, an idea, a next to nothing, a nothing; the French say a *soupçon*, a suspicion: that is, one should suspect it's there but not be certain.

The finest example of vagueness is found in a recipe of Maestro Martino, a famous Como cook of the fifteenth century, in fact the most famous Italian cook of that century. The recipe, perhaps too elementary to appear in an illustrious recipe book, is for soft-boiled eggs: "Put fresh eggs in boiling water and boil them as long as it takes to say an Our Father," Martino writes, using a measure of time that was in keeping with his job as cook for the patriarch of Aquileia, and was quite common in those days when clocks were scarce.

With a clock it's simpler. And yet even so one can make a mistake. The absentminded Newton wanted to make a hard-boiled egg. He put a pot of water on the fire; on the table he had the egg ready; in his hand he held the clock to time the cooking. When the water began to boil, Newton, thinking of other things as he watched, threw in the clock.

A new method of writing recipes appeared in the *New Yorker* of January 13, 1975. In a drawing by Ed Koren there is a woman in the kitchen, spoon in hand, in front of a large pot and an open cookbook. She is reading a recipe.

> In a large bowl, combine 60¢ of eggs, 45¢ of medium cream, 16¢ of oregano, and 10¢ of dry mustard. Dip $7.50 of loin pork chops into this mixture and roll in 65¢ of bread crumbs. Heat 90¢ of peanut oil in a heavy skillet and slowly fry the chops on 94¢ of gas.

⟃ XIX ⟄

To Maestro Martino Como has dedicated a street near the old Contrada (Street) of Flowers, where I was born. The Contrada of Flowers was later called Via Santo Garovaglio, not a saint but a naturalist of the nineteenth century, a "happy investigator of nature," in the footsteps of Pliny the Elder, who, along with Pliny the Younger, makes up the most ancient pair of illustrious citizens of Como. To Alessandro Volta, the inventor of potato gnocchi as well as of the *pila* (galvanic battery), Como has dedicated a square, a monument, and a temple beside the lake.

I turn onto Via Maestro Martino, a narrow street that slopes upward slightly and ends at an old trattoria, unfortunately "renovated."

I go in. The dining room is empty, it's just eleven, the only activity is in the kitchen. Who knows, perhaps as a child I was brought here one Sunday for lunch by my father, who was baptized Tomaso but called Paolino by everyone. An old cook leans out of a small arched service hatch, with a white cap on his head; he greets me kindly.

I tell him about Martino, who left a book of recipes.

"One could take up some of the dishes, follow some of his suggestions. For example, on fried *agoni*" — "*ces petits poissons dont les Comasques sont si fiers*" (the little fish that people in Como are so proud of), as a friend of Garovaglio's once said — "Martino recommends squeezing orange juice rather than lemon. What do you think?"

The old man shakes his tall white cap.

"It's not the season for *agoni* now."

"What do you think of naming a street after a cook? Doesn't it seem to you that the city of Como has had an intelligent and civilized idea?"

The old man shakes his hat again.

"No," he says; he thinks a moment, then concludes: "A cook is only a servant."

Ah me, this disdain a cook has for his profession saddens me, even if it's just the outburst of a moment. Going back to his work the cook invites me to return when the *agoni* are in season, so we can try them with orange juice.

I go out of the restaurant. But I am no longer in Via Maestro Martino. In reality this street doesn't exist in Como. There is Via Santo Garovaglio, there is the lake, rimmed with floating debris, the sun, the funicular that goes up, but no Via Maestro Martino. There is not even a monument to the Maestro, a monument similar to the one dedicated to Alessandro Volta: Martino represented standing with a fork in his hand, atop a high pedestal on which are shown in bas-relief the implements of his art: pots, grills, ladles, and *missoltitt* (dried *agoni*), onions, spring onions . . . a monument that because of the fork recalls Baron Brisse, a famous French gourmet, of whom Monselet says: "Death surprised him with fork in hand."

It would be the only monument to a cook in the world, since the simple marble bust erected — *par souscription publique et mondiale* in the little town of Villeneuve-Loubet, near Nice — in honor of Auguste Escoffier, gentleman, restorer of French cuisine, and inventor of peach Melba, is not a true monument. Not even the monument set in the center of the lovely Place Stanislas, in Nancy, in honor of Stanislaus I Leszczynski, the inventor of *baba au rhum*, can be considered a true monument to a cook: Stanislaus was also the king of Poland twice, then the duke of Lorena and the father-in-law of Louis XV, who invented the omelette with asparagus tips.

The train leaving Como travels slowly along one of the main streets of the city, as if it were in America; the jolts are muffled by the red velvet of first class, with the embroidered cover for the head. Farewell, royal city of *missoltitt*, and town of the onions. Farewell, my fellow citizens, freshwater sailors and mountaineers of the plain. The Palazzo Terragni, rationalist dream of the Como architect Terragni, passes wavering before my eyes; rising steeply behind it is the mountain of Brunate, Como's acropolis, where the place of the Parthenon is occupied by the former annex of the Hotel Milano, whose facade, faded by the distance, sticks up continuously above the roofs of the city. The duomo goes by, and the famous frog, carved in the fifteenth century by the brothers Tommaso and Jacopo Rodari (by which of the two we will never know) and decapitated by a fanatic with a hammer in 1912: which should be seen not, as some believe, as a mark of the level reached by the lakewater during a big flood, or as a descendant of the large tadpole carved in the bottom of one of the holy-water basins in the duomo, but, as the back legs, which seem to be extended in a spasm, clearly indicate, as the prefiguration of the frog of Galvani, who was to open the way to the artificial electric organ, later called *appareil à colonne,* then *appareil à pile,* and finally *pile.* And here again are the white neon lights of the ancient Cinema Plinio (the Elder), and, almost at the end of the street, the mysterious sign of the Silenzio restaurant: as if the blessed god of silence himself, the boy Arpocrates, were to suddenly appear among the laid tables in his usual pose, with the index finger of his right hand on his lips.

NOTES ON TRAVEL

❦

From Ciudad de Mexico
to Riobamba (1956)

CIUDAD DE MEXICO

Tibón, who is from Como, travels everywhere, even in the *selva*, the rain forest, carrying only a box of grated Parmesan cheese, which he sprinkles on whatever he is given to eat. Tibón's information: in Ticúl are the Xiú, descendants of the Mayan kings. The Xiú live like peasants, in huts. For Mérida: the first ferry is in Tuxpan; the second in Tecolutla; just beyond the river is the shack of Fortunato Nochebuena, a former ship's cook, who prepares an excellent seviche served on massive mahogany tables. In Mérida remember to have the *sopa de lima* at the Dos Tulipancitos restaurant.

At the mechanic's on Avenida Cuautemoc. On Avenida San Juan de Letrán people stretched out on the sidewalk reading the newspaper. Take what's needed for sterilizing syringes. Copy the map of the *selva* Lacandona from the book by Franz Blom. Gifts for the Lacandon: canvas hammocks (fifteen dollars), gargantillas (beads) for the women, salt, coffee, aspirin. In Tenosique speak with Plinio Valenzuela, *empresario chiclero* (chewing-gum trader).

> *Things to buy:*
> Petromax
> toilet paper
> salt
> saucepan
> Bacardi
> bags
> shoes
> dextrose
> hard-boiled eggs
> cases of mineral water

Just outside Acapulco, on the road to Mexico City, look for a little restaurant with a garden called El Parque Cachù. The proprietor, a fellow with gray hair and a Mexican wife, known as the gringo, is B. (Bruno?) Traven, the mysterious author of *The Bridge in the Jungle*. To Huston, who shot *The Treasure of the Sierra Madre* (another of his books), he presented himself as Hal Croves, Traven's secretary.

Guatemala

Flight over the Mayan ruins in the *selva*. Landing in Puerto Barrios, on the Atlantic, to pick up the colonel-pilot's clean laundry. Tropical city, big wooden houses green, yellow, gray, with verandas, high-ceilinged rooms, blacks, malaria.

Cigarettes: Payasos, King Bee, Victór: *fume Victór, es mejor*. In Iztapa, on the Pacific, ranchos (boardinghouses) on the spit of sand.

> Rancho Michatoya
> IztapaDesayunos
> Almuerzos
> Cenas
> Pescado frito

Huevos
Caldo de pescado
Frijoles
Café
Tortillas
Cervezas
Aguas gaseosas
Gramizadas
Cocos
Cigarros

The full moon, the white stakes in the lagoon, the two men working at night, the fires on the banks to smoke out the mosquitoes. Outboards and *cayucos*, night swim, *tiburones* (sharks).

Chichicastenango, that is, the place of nettles. Pension Chiguilá. The two little Indians hired to clean the birds. When the birds escape they recapture them, drenching them with water. The bird's stupidity: when the door of the cage opens it stays on the threshold, hopping up and down without going anywhere; when it finally gets out, it makes a short flight and returns to the cage.

At the Mayan Inn the child bartender mixes daiquiris for the tourists.

Ciudad de Guatemala. *Carnicería* (butcher shop) la Predilecta (the Favorite). *Servicio urbano de autobuses. Guarde este boleto para entregarlo al Inspector cuando se lo pida, y destruyalo al bajar del autobus.* (Keep this ticket to show to the inspector when he asks and destroy it when you get off the bus.)

Dinner at the ambassador's. An enormous silver plate: yellow risotto *alla milanese* with truffles from Kabul, Afghanistan, the former residence of the ambassador. Cigarettes: Casino, Delicados, Elegantes.

El Salvador

Principal cities: Santa Ana, San Miguel, San Vicente, Santa Rosa, Santa Tecla, San Salvador, *la capital*. One dollar equals two and a half colones. Cigarettes: Embajadores. Presidential candidate: Lemus.

Honduras

Tegucigalpa, Hotel Boston. One dollar equals two lempiras. Cigarettes: King Bee, King Bee extra, Dorados. Rain of fishes in Yoro, in late May. The slaughterhouse at the end of the valley below the bridge, with oxen that refuse to enter and hundreds of vultures flying overhead.

Servicio aéreo de Honduras. Destino: Ruinas de Copán. The plane lands at San Pedro Sula, the beautiful young woman gets out. The new airplane is full of peasants and chicken cages. Santa Barbara, Santa Rosa de Copán, and Copán Ruinas. Beyond the stony runway is the path to the Mayan ruins, a cut through the forest: the orange trees planted by the archaeologists are loaded with fruit. The boardinghouse is in the town, up on the hill.

The rectangular square with the Lux bar, the coconut palms, the polished concrete pavement of the arcades, the white houses, the bridge and the washerwomen below, the football field, the Mayan stele along the dusty road, the veiled sky, the loud cicadas, the dry leaves that men sweep away into big piles. A haze veils the whole countryside. At the Lux, on returning, we drink everything in sight: orange juice, a bottle of lemonade, a carton of chocolate drink, beer, and *tiste*: water with sugar and cinnamon, beaten with a whisk under the eyes of the bitch Coqueta (Coquette), a cross between a wolf, Policía (Police), and a dachshund, Salsicia (Sausage).

Incident at the border with Nicaragua, where a double visit takes place: customs at El Espino and passports at Somoto, the official there stops working at noon. Drinks: violet, emerald green, pink.

Nicaragua

Night in Managua, Hotel Lido Palace *a las orillas*, on the shores, of the Lago de Managua, with an illuminated green pool, cold tea, and grapefruit. Manager, Colonel H. J. Perron. Everywhere soldiers in German-style uniforms, polished boots, officials standing stiff around the billiard table, holding their cues like weapons.

One dollar equals six and a quarter colones. Discussion at the dinner table: *El hombre cuanto mas tiene pelo mas mono es.* (The more hair a man has the closer to a monkey he is.)

Costa Rica

San José, Hotel Ritz. In the lobby the Cuban with the electric guitar plays to himself day and night. Fabian Dobles, the writer — *oficina near Ciudadela del Zapote, preguntar en la pulperia* (ask in the drugstore) *Buenavista* — prefers to work after five. At the Soda Palace, Parque Central, Antonio Menendez, referred to by Pacho de la Espriella, offers a *leche malteada*: malted milk. Cigarettes: Leon, Ticos, Virginia. Dobles: the story of General Sandino, a professor. He goes to the peace talks with Somoza, as he leaves he is machine-gunned. Gregg commercial school across from the Ritz. From early morning to midnight the classrooms are filled with girls, white, black, and mixed. Many people always waiting outside.

Addresses in San José, where the houses are not numbered: Señor X, *barrio* (neighborhood) Moravia, 75 *varras al norte de la bomba de gasolina*, on the left, new yellow and red house. Or: barrio Escalante, 400 *varras al sur de la pulperia La Luz* on the *carretera San Pedro*.

Info Ecuador. King Otaval, ended up on the Spanish grill. Remains of the Incas near Quito. Monument to the equator. One dollar equals two sucres. The hats called Panama (*sombreros Panamá*), which in fact are made in Ecuador. Emeralds.

Departure for Panama. Vain search for Sancho at home and at the Ministerio del Trabajo and for the forty dollars left in his pocket. Six-hour wait at the airport, the rainy season begins, din of rain on the sheet-metal roof.

Panama

Panama, city of fish. Hotel Colón: green, wooden, lopsided, with small dark courtyards, the old porter who doesn't understand. Brief warm showers. Sound of domino players in the cafés. One dollar equals two balboa. Fruit: chico zapote, *aguacate*, mango, *maní* (peanuts), banana: *plátano* (to be cooked) and *guineo; naranja, piña* (pineapple), *toronja* (grapefruit), *caña.*

Ecuador

The plane lands in Guayaquil, on the coast. The Guayas River winds endlessly through swampland before reaching the ocean. Lobsters that taste of mud. A seven-hour flight to the Galápagos Islands.

Quito, Hotel Majestic. Departure in the Land Rover of Chavez, Ecuadorian employee of the embassy. Ambassador: "Get going, you animal!" Chavez: "Thank you, Excellency!" Torrential rain on mountains of green bananas thrown away on the shore of the Esmeralda River. Hotel Las Palmas, owned by a former Italian sailor arrested in Genoa in 1918 for singing:

> *El General Cadorna*
> *El mangia el bev el dorma . . .*

(General Cadorna / eats, drinks, and sleeps . . . He was the Italian commander in chief during the Great War, 1915–18, until Caporetto.)

Santo Domingo de los Colorados, Hotel Astoria, with bar. Search for a towel. Roulette wheels in the square in front of the hotel, like market stalls, crowded with players.

Inspection by Land Rover toward the Colorados, the car ends up in the mud. On foot to the house of Porfirio Salazacón, the chief of the Colorados. He's not home. Return on foot to the Astoria. Half a bottle of Pernod found in the bar.

Again to the Colorados, on horseback. Wait until three in the afternoon, when they return from hunting. Again wait. Negotiations. The chicken, tied to the saddle near the fire where it will be cooked, stands on only one leg, like a swamp bird. Opening the *latas* (cans). Dinner. Balsa-wood bed with blanket stinking of horses. Porfirio's two clients (he is a healer). Contract. Music. Opening the bottles of *aguardiente.*

Riobamba. Indians swarming in the streets, always running with short steps, carrying heavy weights. Long dirty black hair, coarse as horsehair, yellow eyes. Riding on the roof of the train. The old women spin wool as they go along . . .

*From New York to Charleston,
South Carolina, and back (1956)*

NEW YORK, MONDAY, FEBRUARY 8
 The Cadillac comes out of the tunnel under the Hudson and takes the highway heading south. The skyscrapers disappear into the fog. A fine dusty snow begins to fall; it doesn't stick on the ground.

Soon we are in the woods. Oaks and small cypresses: trees felled by the wind and rotting on the ground, dead trees standing, their trunks white, without bark. The houses are more and more infrequent, most of them wooden, the majority painted white, or yellow with white trim, a few are brick, others have fake brick or fake stone facades. The snow begins to stick. White sky, white fields, white houses, black windows. Red and blue on the gas stations and motel signs. We leave the big highway; two cannons in a meadow mark an old battlefield. In Lambertville, we stop to eat: eggs and bacon, beer, coffee.

At nightfall we reach Gettysburg. The square, covered with snow, reflects the lights. Gettysburg Hotel: wide, comfortable bed, restful lights, dark wall-to-wall carpeting, double window; beyond the glass, house fronts illuminated by red neon. We have dinner at the hotel: leg of lamb with mint jelly, potatoes, beans, lettuce, coffee.

After dinner a visit to the Old Wills House, filled with souvenirs of Lincoln: photographs, paintings, a lock of hair, Lincoln's friend, Lincoln's valet, the chair where Lincoln sat, and finally the big bed, with embroidered white pillows, where Lincoln slept before delivering, at the National Cemetery, the Gettysburg Address. The custodian, an old man in shirtsleeves, points out with an ebony cane all the objects on display, not missing a single one. Perhaps accustomed to groups of tourists whose attention wanders, he breaks the monotony of his lecture by occasionally raising the tone of his voice with a violence that finds no echo on his impassive face.

When we leave, Gettysburg is deserted. Silence of the snow. Neatly painted houses, polished brass. From the Masonic hall comes the dull crash of bowling balls. Lighted windows along the sidewalk. Through venetian blinds, in one living room after another, people rest, read, and, above all, watch television.

Gettysburg, Pennsylvania, Tuesday, February 9

Breakfast in the room: coffee, toast, butter, orange marmalade. Out the window, beyond the roofs of the houses, the hills and forests that had been hidden by darkness.

Leaving Gettysburg, we go through the Civil War battlefields, which are maintained as parks, and have a lot of monuments, columns, obelisks, marble and bronze statues, steles, plaques, cannons scattered about. Endless forest; few houses but always supplied with cars; bogs in the forest.

When we get to Washington, the snow disappears. In the sun we drive through the suburbs, an immense parkland strewn with large houses.

The White House just repainted, the Capitol, big lawns, air.

The long, comfortable lobby of the Mayflower Hotel, rows of rooms with tables set for banquets. We eat in a Chinese restaurant crowded with office workers: grilled pork cutlets with sweet sauce and mustard, vegetables, coffee.

On the streets American faces and hats more numerous than in New York. Cowboy hats: refined, but always with taller crowns and wider brims than normal hats; the taxis smaller.

Street of entertainment: striptease, playland, movieland; a girl trying on bra, stockings, and panties in three dimensions, ten cents.

The weather becomes more pleasant, the houses more neglected. A big swamp with burned tree trunks sticking up out of it, landscape of disaster: but only for a moment. Aluminum silos sparkling in the sun, cemeteries without fences, gravestones among the trees, in the grass, white plantation houses from the days of Uncle Tom, still surrounded by the small dark-log cabins of the slaves; and on every porch wooden rocking chairs or mass-produced metal ones, red or yellow.

Fredericksburg. Monroe's house, small, brick, very low, very comfortable, with a little garden behind and an old cemetery, and, scattered throughout the city, imitations (but larger) of Monroe's house.

In Richmond, because of a convention, there are no rooms in the hotels. We continue on toward Petersburg. The sun sets behind the woods but the light lingers, as in summer. Motels, motor courts, trailer parks, gas stations, strings of lights above used-car lots, neon lights, lighted signs, automobile headlights brighter and brighter against the darkening sky. Petersburg, Petersburg Hotel.

Dinner at the hotel: pepper soup, veal cutlet with green beans and potatoes, coffee. First, however, a delightful black girl dressed in white (the waitress) comes to offer an antipasto. The rest of the meal is served by a Negro waiter, and the girl works at the back of the dining room. Even her legs, the danger area for a black woman, are shapely from the knees down. A beauty, with an intense, reserved gaze.

Sycamore Street. The brightly lighted white tower of the courthouse, pool halls. We look in the windows and immediately the patrons turn to look at us. Negro neighborhood, dark streets, lit-up shopwindows. In one window living-room furniture is displayed: a shiny pedestal with a shelf on top for cigarettes and an ashtray with a big lighter, and, above the shelf, a lamp. For the wall: a clock in the shape of a cat with a tail that oscillates like a pendulum and eyes that look this way and that with the beats of the tail. Patent leather and snakeskin shoes, brilliant shirts. A Chinese man, motionless in the half-dark laundry among piles of linens, listens to music on records that we cannot hear. A well-dressed white man comes up to us with shaky steps and asks for money. At nine, three ladies come out of a big cafeteria; they are the last customers.

The water faucets on the sink are spring mounted: if you take your hand off they stop. At night a constant noise of pipes: pounding, tapping. I close the radiators because it is too hot, but the steam leaks from the valve, hissing.

Petersburg, Virginia, Wednesday, February 10

The Negro waiter enters with breakfast: scrambled eggs, orange juice, glass of ice water, coffee, jam, butter, toast. I raise the blinds: good weather, the sun is strong coming through the dirty glass (the blinds do not usually go up).

At midday we stop in Henderson, a small silent place in the sun, where the railroad passes through. Slightly shabby hotel, white columns, high ceiling with big black fans, still waiting for summer. Vegetable soup, dried-out pork cutlets, and apple pie that's too sweet. The train, with its big freight cars colored like toys, advances slowly between the low houses ringing its bell, and goes by a few feet from our table.

In these woods, as soon as the houses disappear, it's as if one could be anywhere. Then suddenly a factory surrounded by cars appears, or a school, or a car dealer, among the trees. The driver breaks his long silence to call our attention to a mule that a farmer is using for plowing, an unusual sight. We go by Raleigh and arrive in Greensboro, the King Cotton Hotel.

Dinner at the hotel. A cute young woman serves us, thin, with a child-size head that makes her seem taller. She ignores our looks. Her arms are a little too thin, angular, a slight defect, at least at first glance, and fairly common among Americans. Perhaps the price of their extremely shapely legs. Or, rather, this slenderness will be attractive to me when I have been completely invaded by the American horror of fat.

After dinner a walk on Main Street, lit up like all Main Streets. Beside the polished granite base of a bank a line of Negroes wait for the bus that will take them to their dark neighborhood. A drunk goes by, supported by a cop, his head extended toward us with excessive courtesy, as if to start a conversation.

Here, in 1862, William Sydney Porter was born; that is, O. Henry.

Greensboro, North Carolina, Thursday, February 11

Gray sky. A Negro with thin features brings breakfast: coffee in a thermos-coffeepot, glass of ice water, orange juice, jam, butter, two pieces of toast, and a big, very soft paper napkin.

We leave Greensboro by way of the Negro section. Negroes standing in groups on the sidewalk, leaning against the wall. They're talking, or simply standing in the sun. A very black Negress, with two tight braids, dressed completely in black. Another, fat, with short blue jeans and a long purple silk jacket. A young man in pressed white pants, a bit long over black shoes, and a gray canvas flight jacket. Men's hats of white and yellow felt. A yellow bus goes by, crowded with black heads.

The road is cut into the red earth, between expanses of dry grass scattered with wild cypresses. One searches involuntarily for an order in their arrangement, an order that, of course, does not exist.

We pass an old wooden building that looks like a pagoda and turn back to have a look. The house that it belongs to is in ruins. A farmer arrives on his tractor, we can go in and look around, it's all for sale. The furniture, of a style vaguely Art Nouveau, is broken, and so are the fixtures, the paintings. Boxes of books and letters in disarray, books scattered on the floor under the dust. Two young men, his sons, accompany us. They look around with amazement, as if they had come in here for the first time.

We also visit the pagoda, now used as a stable and garage, perhaps once used for tobacco. A car without tires, raised up on blocks for a long rest, is in one corner. Behind the pagoda a grove of evergreens with a gravel path and tombstones: the family graveyard.

Concord, cotton industry, shopwindows full of sheets and towels, white, pink, blue. In the restaurant a table of gesticulating old ladies, of Scottish origin. Vegetable soup, hamburger, blueberry pie, coffee. No beer, dry town.

Charlotte, Selwyn Hotel. The elevator girl: freckled face, shiny olive-green silk ribbon in her shiny hair, green dress, blue jacket.

We sit down in the New Yorker Restaurant, but it doesn't serve beer. The waitress reluctantly points out the nearest restaurant with, possibly, beer, the Piedmont Restaurant, where we eat vegetable soup, Virginia ham with pineapple — one of the best dishes in American cooking — and coffee. We drink the beer with more pleasure than usual.

Long, narrow movie theater, feet resting on the backs of the seats in front, loud laughter. Two cartoons, one installment of a serial (the continuation the following week), a Western. All without intermission, as always.

Another beer in the room.

Charlotte, North Carolina, Friday, February 12

Clear sparkling morning. The lighted neon as red as coals on the black backgrounds of the signs. The enormous shadow of a skyscraper over the low roofs. From my window I see four skyscrapers: one gray concrete, one white, one yellow, one red. The dominant color is a sooty brick-red. White and red facades. Red, green, blue, yellow, black signs. Huge writing in paint on empty walls. In the background the forest.

On the chest of drawers a Bible: "The Holy Bible placed by the Gideons. Authorized (King James) version." At the end of the volume is a list of readings for every day of the year. For today, February 12, I read: "An eleven-day journey."

Columbia. Wide sidewalks that go uphill and down, streets lined with shop signs, plate glass in the sun, clear sky. In front of the gas station the first palm trees. Midday silence, footsteps can be heard on the sidewalk. Pool, flippers, movieland: faded brownish film — a girl in a canoe, standing, back turned, moves her oar and her behind to keep her balance.

Jefferson Hotel. In the men's room a fellow is shaving. Very high-ceilinged dining room, light filtering through the venetian blinds. We order ham and macaroni, fried chicken, corn, potatoes, beer, coffee. Between the order and the arrival of the food more time than usual passes.

Negro section. The streets are very wide even here, but not paved. Red, compacted earth; crooked little houses are crowded along the sidewalk that goes uphill. S. finds it difficult (impossible) to draw Negroes. A duel with unequal weapons.

Between Columbia and Charleston woods, farms, immense fields cut out of the forest. Beside one house a vegetable garden, the only one seen so far. Cows with long, disheveled orange-spotted coats, some huge trees, perhaps sycamores. Endless straight roads on the rolling landscape, entire woods covered with Spanish moss, long gray beards that transform the trees into phantoms. A wide river cuts through the forest: trees up to the water's edge, the last ones lean into the river.

In North Charleston this wilderness ends. Divided highway with a wide strip between the two sides, houses, motels, tracks, factories, ravaged palm trees, big car-graveyards, a mountain of old yellowed refrigerators. Bundles of telegraph wires, shining reservoirs, the low sun's long shadows, smoke, light, sea air. Houses closer together, bicycles on the porches. In Charleston the street narrows. Shopwindows, stores, neon, more and more lights. King Street, the main street, is narrow and very long. Old white-painted wooden houses mixed in with the modern blocks of stores, restaurants, movie theaters. Negroes, sailors, Chinese, college students, cadets in uniform. The last stretch, with no shops, is darker. Old brick houses with their dates in view on the pediments, books, paintings, prints behind the lighted windows.

Finally, a big field strewn with trees in an orderly way, like an olive grove, and the sea. It's almost night and the water is dark.

The horizon is closed off by a long wooded island. Looks like the lagoon of Venice.

Fort Sumter Hotel, big green building for tourists, not for business travelers. I go to the window thinking I'll see the sea but it faces the city: a mass of old roofs neatly painted black, red, green, gray, with the glare of King Street on the white facades.

We go out for dinner. The pleasure of old architecture, together with the oppressiveness of restorations, of things officially catalogued as beautiful, untouchable, and destined to eternal life, against nature. Immense pool halls, dancing schools. Beautiful cashiers in their crystal cages at the movie theaters. Bars darker than in New York, in the darkness sailors and girls sitting in a row at the bar. One girl, back turned to us, is dancing, her head beautifully drawn under hair a little too peroxided. Delicate, slender legs that she moves artfully a few inches at a time gliding on her flat-heeled shoes.

Dinner: shrimp and rice Portuguese style, cottage cheese and cut-up pineapple on a slice of tomato placed on a lettuce leaf.

Charleston, South Carolina, Saturday, February 13

Sun, pale sky, like September. We head north along the sea. The big bridge at the end of the street looks, in perspective, like a tower. Flat land, straight, taller than usual pines, sunlight suffuses the clearings. Negroes' dark cabins on the dry grass, oil cans in the sun, laundry, a wooden fenced enclosure with a mule who is sunning himself. Mailboxes on the edge of the forest where there are no houses. Arms of the sea, bridges, stretches of swamp grass. A pelican flies away heavily.

We turn right, toward the sea hidden by the dunes. Vacation cottages on pilings, all closed up, there is no one in the whole village. The ocean waves break with a loud roar on the beach of white, sugarlike sand that extends as far as the eye can see.

Myrtle Beach: greenish-blue palms and a lot of white in the houses and the shops scattered along the beach. We eat at the back of the restaurant, far from the sparkle of the sun's reflections.

Wilmington, Cape Fear Hotel. The room has double doors, one of which is a shutter that lets the air circulate, so when it's very hot you can sleep with the other door open. The harbor is on the wide estuary of Cape Fear. Smell of fresh water. Brick warehouses, huge iron girders painted bright red, the fireboat. No traffic, it's Saturday.

Dinner at the hotel. It's eight, already late. The few people eat in silence, the waitress puts the napkin on my lap. Potato soup, tasteless shrimp, salad, beer, coffee.

We drop in at a kind of popular theater, a long hall adapted as a theater, with old seats. Thick smell of popcorn, people changing places constantly. Banjo, guitar, double bass, violin, accordion, singing; a clown, a master of ceremonies. A little boy in front of me is never still, his head continuously swings against the background of the stage.

We go on to a movie theater. The film is set in California, very like the landscape we saw today in Myrtle Beach. The darkness, the screen, the seats, the sound of the loudspeaker are the same all over the world, Edward G. Robinson is an old acquaintance. For a moment I thought I was in Italy; and then immediately the sensation of being at a great distance from Italy.

Wilmington, North Carolina, Sunday, February 14

The winter sun has a hard time coming out in the half-clouded sky, but it's warm. Churches with open doors, shoe-shine boys at work. The car stops under the trees on Market Street, opposite an old colonial mansion. Sunday silence. Birds, distant voices; cars pass us at regular intervals with the muffled roar of waves on the beach.

New Bern: a vaguely Swiss air hovers over the city. We eat at the Queen Anne Hotel: white columns, red wall-to-wall, mahogany, mirrors, soft, slightly funereal pop music. It's hot, only one other customer in the dining room.

The host leads us silently to a table near a window; beyond the glass is a flowering shrub whose red petals are being eaten by swallows. A tall waitress, smiling, with fat, unshapely legs, brings salad, chicken with mushrooms, boiled potatoes, corn, coffee; then she withdraws to a corner of the room. She yawns, sees that she is observed, smiles. The host slowly approaches the table and delicately picks up a piece of lettuce that has fallen on the carpet.

At sunset we arrive in Norfolk, full of short seamen and naval police with big white sticks. Monticello Hotel, room with television, you hear the one in the next room. Dinner in the hotel: soup with vermicelli, cold meat, beer, coffee. Up to now no fruit.

Norfolk, Virginia, Monday, February 15

Williamsburg, old Colonial city restored and in large part reconstructed by John D. Rockefeller (forty-five million dollars), today populated by about seven thousand people, some of whom go around in eighteenth-century costume, and by a crowd of tourists who at midday disperse to thirty or so restaurants.

Chicken, sweet potatoes, beer, coffee. Beautiful fields, low brick walls and wooden fences, tall trees soften the severity of the reconstruction. A little ways from downtown we come to the romantic Eastern State Hospital, founded in 1770, the oldest mental hospital in the United States.

Richmond, King Karter Hotel. In the hurry of leaving the hotel I forget to ask for information about King Karter.

Before it gets dark we are in time to see the first White House of the Confederacy. The street ends in a kind of lookout over an industrial valley and hills covered with houses. Smoke from the chimneys restfully veils the red light of sunset. At the restaurant: shrimp, lobsters, and coleslaw, the appetizing cabbage salad.

Richmond, Virginia, Tuesday, February 16

Sun. Stop in Farmville to eat. Summer awnings on the shops; barbers; shoe-shine boys. The breeze makes the stockings on the skinny legs of an old Negro woman flap. We go into a restaurant but it's too hot. At the local hotel: tomato sauce, scrambled eggs with brains, coffee.

Lynchburg, Virginia Hotel. One always seems to arrive at the same hotel: black man who takes the bags, carpets, elevator with Negro woman, corridors, fire escape, Bible. Too hot. I open the window: low gray clouds; the warm wind carries a good scent of rain into the room.

Lynchburg, Virginia, Wednesday, February 17

We head toward the mountains: frequent curves, isolated, the houses less ornate, made of real stone; it's cool. The fields are full of stones, yet there is more under cultivation than in other places where the earth appears more fertile.

Monticello, the house that Jefferson built on a hilltop, is visited as a museum. So is the nearby Ash Lawn, Monroe's house, also built by Jefferson (who was an architect) but smaller, modest: an ideal house. You note that it is the same man of the little house in Fredericksburg; surely Monroe must have liked staying home.

When we finish eating we go back to the car. The driver has just lighted a splendid Havana cigar but, when we arrive, he throws it away without the least appearance of displeasure and sits behind the wheel.

Hagerstown, a German city: steak with applesauce, cabbage, lots of butter. Chorus of old men behind a window, on the street. Long houses, no longer in vertical sections, no cubelike shops with big plate-glass windows. Streets of houses and stores mixed together.

The main hotel is full. We sleep at the Colonial, narrow corridors, room without bath, bed comfortable and clean as usual. No Bible.

Hagerstown, Maryland, Thursday, February 18

Baltimore: rich countryside, cultivated in big expanses, farms where one would like to live, excellent road. We eat in a restaurant by the side of the road: eggs and bacon, fried potatoes, beer. We return to the highway that we took when we left. Factories, refineries; bridges and viaducts that intersect, and cross over marshes. Behind the hills that hide the Hudson the skyscrapers of Manhattan stick up and shift on the horizon like the moon. Coming out of the tunnel under the river we are suddenly in New York, home. On the sidewalk there is a big leather armchair still in good condition. It will not be easy to break it up and get it onto the garbage truck.

The trip lasted eleven days, exactly as it was written in the Bible at the Selwyn Hotel.

$\mathcal{N}otes$

INTRODUCTION

Page 3

The brown poodle Butz, who comes back to life for a moment at the beginning of this piece, is mentioned in a letter from Desmond McCarthy to Bertrand Russell, who reports it in his autobiography. Another of Schopenhauer's poodles — called Atma, which in Sanskrit means "Soul of the world" — is depicted, in a woodcut of the time, in the act of staring intensely at the face of his master, who, with his white hair cut like a poodle's, stands holding his chin between thumb and index finger, meditating. Schopenhauer's final walking companion, whom he called one of his best friends, was a black poodle. The visitor who knocked at the philosopher's door immediately heard barking; entering, he saw the walls decorated almost entirely with portraits of dogs. "If there were no dogs," the Master once said, "I would not want to live." And it seems that on one of the rare occasions when he had to scold one of his poodles he used these words: "You're no better than a man!"

Page 3

"Dante says": Paradiso, XIII 139

Page 11
"A novel full of passion": Marcel Proust, from an undated letter to his friend Robert de Flers.

Page 12
"the Bohemian Cigar Divan by T. Godall": Robert Louis Stevenson. *The Dynamiter.*

Page 14
"raven-haired": Isaac Babel, *Red Calvary.*

NOTES ON LIFE

Page 45
"as Proust says": Marcel Proust, *The Past Recaptured*

NOTES ON GASTRONOMY

Page 52
Anthelme Brillat-Savarin, *The Physiology of Taste, or Meditations on Transcendental Gastronomy*, Part I, Meditation IV.

Page 52
The Art of Cooking in the Nineteenth Century: See Jean Paul Aron, *The Art of Eating in France: Manners and Menus in the Nineteenth Century*, New York, Harper & Row, 1975.

Page 55
Atheneus of Naucratis, *The Deipnosophists.*

Page 55
Jean de La Bruyère, *Les Caractères ou les Moeurs de ce Siècle.*

Page 55
John Updike: Mimi Sheraton, "John Updike Ruminates on Matters Gustatory," *New York Times*, December 15, 1982.

Page 58
"Cooking is done . . . .": Gino Scarpa, *Colloqui con Arturo Martini* [Conversations with Arturo Martini], XIII, Rizzoli, Milano, 1968.

Page 58
"Take eight two-day old eggs . . . ": *Opera* di Bartolomeo Scappi, maestro dell'arte del cucinare, con Ia quale si può ammaestrare qualsivoglia cuoco, scalco, trinciante o maestro di casa. Divisa in sei libri . . . Con le figure che fanno di bisogno nella cucina [Works, by Bartolomeo Scappi, master of the culinary art, by means of which any cook, carver, slicer, or steward can be trained. Divided into six books . . . With the necessary illustrations] . . . Alessandro de' Vecchi, Venezia, 1622.

Page 59
"*carneplastico*": F.T. Marinetti and Fillia, *La Cucina Futurista*, Sonzogno, Milano, 1932.

Page 60
Apicius, *De re coquinaria*, Book IV, Chapter V.

Page 67
Beatus ille . . .": Jospeh Eichendorff, *Memoirs of a Good-for-Nothing*, Chapter 9.

Page 71
Maestro Martino's Work, *Libro de arte coquinaria compsto per lo egregio Maestro Martino coquo olim del reverndissimo monsignor camerlengo et patriarcha de Aquileia* [On the Art of Cooking, compsed by the eminent Maestro Martino former cook of the most Reverend Monsignor Chamberlain and Patriarch of Aquileia], was published for the first time in *Arte della Cucina, Libri di Ricette, Testi sopra lo Scalco, il Trinciante e i Vini, dal XIV al XIX secolo,* [The Art of Cooking, Recipes and Essays on Carving, Slicing, and Wine, from the XIV to the XIX centuries] eidted by Emilio Faccioli. Edizioni Il Polifilo, Milano, 1966.

ABOUT THE AUTHOR

ALDO BUZZI trained as an architect in Milan, where he now lives. He worked in the Italian cinema for many years and then in a publishing house. His writing has appeared in many literary journals and he has had several books published in Italy.

ABOUT THE BOOK

The text for this book was composed by Steerforth Press using a digital version of Electra, a typeface designed in 1935 by William Addison Dwiggins. Electra has been a standard book typeface since its release because of its evenness of design and high legibility. All Steerforth books are printed on acid-free papers and this book was bound by BookCrafters of Chelsea, Michigan.

Other Steerforth Italia Books

OPEN CITY
Seven Writers in Postwar Rome
Edited by William Weaver

THE WOMAN OF ROME
by Alberto Moravia

THE WATCH
by Carlo Levi

JOURNEY TO THE LAND OF THE FLIES
And Other Travels
by Aldo Buzzi

LIFE OF MORAVIA
by Alberto Moravia and Alain Elkann (AVAILABLE SPRING, 2000)

TWO WOMEN
by Alberto Moravia (AVAILABLE SPRING, 2000)

ROME AND A VILLA
by Eleanor Clark (AVAILABLE SPRING, 2000)

LITTLE NOVELS OF SICILY
by Giovanni Verga (AVAILABLE WINTER, 2000)

THE TIME OF INDIFFERENCE
by Alberto Moravia (AVAILABLE SPRING, 2001)